There's No Happy Ending

THE NEW BIZARRO AUTHOR SERIES

PRESENTS

There's No Happy Ending

Tiffany Scandal

Eraserhead Press
Portland, OR

ERASERHEAD PRESS
205 NE BRYANT
PORTLAND, OR 97211

WWW.ERASERHEADPRESS.COM

ISBN: 1-62105-120-X

Printed in the USA.

Editor's Note

There's a lot I love about bizarro fiction, but one of my favorite things is how easily and beautifully bizarro allows authors to blend genres. Two of my most favorite genres that bizarro blends are the two we don't typically expect to merge--horror and love stories or romances.

There's actually a difference between love stories and romances. For one thing, romances tend to have happy endings, often a wedding. Think *Pride and Prejudice.* Love stories tend to not have happy endings. Think *Romeo and Juliet.*

I hate to ruin the ending for by telling you this, but Tiffany Scandal's *There's No Happy Ending* is a love story. And it's a beautiful one.

There's another thing I love about *There's No Happy Ending* and that's how awesome Isobel is. This is a chick who kicks ass throughout an apocalyptic wasteland wearing her wedding dress and combat boots. Fiction in general can always use more amazing, rock star heroines, and bizarro is no different.

So, lace up your combat boots and get ready for an exciting, heartrending ride.

I'm happy to present Tiffany Scandal's book to you as part of the New Bizarro Author Series. This is this author's first book! The NBAS strives to bring new voices in bizarro fiction to our readers. It serves as an opportunity to introduce you to new writers, and to introduce them into the world of being an author. Eraserhead Press is happy to bring new, weird voices to you in the hopes that these authors will prove themselves to be strong members of the bizarro community and continue to entertain you for years to come. The publishing of this book marks the beginning of a one year proving period. Please help support our NBAS writers in their endeavors by telling your friends about their cool new books. This book you hold is only one of several hundred that must be sold in order for this author to continue on her path. We hope you help her along as best as you can. Thank you.

~Spike Marlowe

Acknowledgements

A tremendous thank you to my family, Michael Kazepis, Kevin Shamel, Rose O'Keefe, Carlton Mellick III, Jeff Burk, Cameron Pierce, Spike Marlowe, Vince Kramer, Jim Agpalza, Eric Hammer, Erika Shuehendler, Curt Sobolewski, Britt Galloway, Karen Pride, Erica Danger, Katie Gerloff, James Bartlett, Ryan Mason, Matthew Humphrey, Sam McCanna, Chrissy Horchheimer, Darryl Yu, the bizarro community, David Lynch, Jorge Luis Borges, coffee, and nightmares.

*If everything is imperfect in this imperfect world,
love is the most perfect in its perfect imperfection.*

The Seventh Seal

One
The World Is Sick

I

"Smells like they're burning bodies again."

A warm breeze blew in and brought a sweet, yet acrid odor with it. The evening sun washed the room in orange.

Isobel said, "Damn. And here I was hoping that someone just fucked up their barbecue."

They laughed. She relished being in Dresden's arms. He traced her lips with his thumb. The crow's feet around his eyes deepened. His pupils dilated and a smile spread on his face. She kissed his thumb and a smile spread on her face. She sighed sweetly, thoughts racing. They were in love.

He grabbed her hand and held it to his face. Turned it to kiss her palm. He caressed the engagement ring on her finger and looked deep in her eyes.

"For always," he whispered.

"For forever," she said.

They embraced and turned to the window and watched the smoke rise in the distance.

II

"I won't allow it. You are not marrying that – *that whore!*" spit sprayed through Elise's clenched teeth.

The lounge smelled like mahogany, leather and formaldehyde. Game trophies lined the walls between large bookshelves. Fire crackled in the pit and Dresden stared at his mother with a stone cold expression.

"Her name is Isobel. And she's not a whore." He tried to keep calm and collected, but found himself digging his fingertips into the couch's arm rest.

"She looks like one."

"Fuck this. I'm leaving."

He stood angrily and his mother reached out toward him. "Dresden, my love, I just want what's best for you."

"I love her. I've been in love with her the last seven years."

"She's no good for you and she is no good for this family. Think of what having her as your wife will do to your future. You are my only living child. I will not have you taken away."

Dresden rolled his eyes and reached for his jacket.

His eyes widened. He attempted to process what had just happened and he felt his body tense up. Dresden wanted to retaliate with a punch. He wanted to call her every profane word that had ever existed. He wanted to walk out and never see her again. But he was here for Isobel. This was important to her. Dresden swallowed his pride, amended his posture and used his right hand to wipe the blood and drool from the corner of his mouth. "What gives?"

"What gives? What gives! You show up to my home and tell me you want to marry some tramp, and you speak filth under my roof, in my presence. . ." Her chest heaved as she cried out.

"I came to you because Isobel insisted that I at least attempt to get your blessing before our wedding tomorrow."

"Tomorrow?!"

"Yes, tomorrow. Honestly, I'm fine without you in our lives, but Isobel on the other hand. . ."

"Tosh." She rolled her eyes and crossed her arms over her chest.

"Listen. She's the most amazing person I've ever met and I can't imagine my life without her. As my mother,

I thought you of all people would want me to be happy. I'm telling you now, she makes me happy. If you can't be happy for us, I will gladly walk out that door a stranger to you and this house."

She scoffed, "Some prostitute spread her legs for you and you think it's love."

"Elise!"

She placed a hand over her chest and exhaled in shock. "How dare . . ."

"How dare you! You never gave her a chance. Why?"

"Dresden, she's not worthy of you. She is not like us."

"She's a good person. And you can't even remember her name."

"Yes, I can."

Dresden arched a brow and waited.

". . . Isadora?"

"See?"

"She . . . she's just trying to climb up in the world. Probably forcing you to marry her." Elise looked down. "Dear god, don't tell me she's . . ." She feigned gagging. "Pregnant."

"She's not."

Elise exaggerated a sigh of relief.

"But getting married was my idea. I'm not doing it to piss you off. She's special. Unique. She fills me with warmth and happiness. Makes me whole." He smiled, thinking of her. "There's no one like her." He shook his head and his seriousness returned. "Do I have your blessing or not?"

"Oh, Dresden . . ." His mother's voice trailed and a tear rolled down her cheek. She held her hand to her chest and pursed her lips.

"Very well. Nice knowing you, Elise."

He grabbed his jacket and headed back for the door. He stopped and turned around. Walked to her crystal glass of vodka tonic on the end table, beside where she had been sitting. He knocked over her drink with a quick, firm swipe. The glass shattered.

"Dresden." Her eyes went wide and she froze where she stood.

"That's for your filthy personality, bitch." He winked at her and walked away.

"Dresden!"

The door slammed shut behind him.

III

The door burst open and Dresden stormed in. "Isobel, fuck it, let's get married tonight."

"So the conversation with your mother went well, huh?" Isobel sat on the bed, surrounded by a collection of magazines and old hardcover books.

Dresden stopped and sighed. He let himself fall on the bed with Isobel. He looked up at her, "Is it weird that I was secretly hoping she'd come around? Mothers should want their children to be happy, right?"

She ran her fingers through his hair. "In a perfect world, yes. But this world's not perfect. We will always have battles to fight, but as long as we love each other, we can stand our own ground."

He smiled up at Isobel, "I love you so much."

"I love you," Isobel returned the smile.

"You sure you don't want to get married tonight?"

"And piss off your mother even more?" Isobel laughed. "She knows when the wedding will be. Let's just stick to the plan. And who knows? Maybe she'll come around in the last minute. We have the rest of our lives to be married. The world's not ending tomorrow."

Isobel smirked in a way that made Dresden melt every time. He rose up to kiss her and she leaned in and pulled his head forward with her hands and used her elbows to push him back against the bed. She climbed on top and straddled him,

"Tomorrow, husband and wife." Dresden lay shirtless on the tousled bed. Looked at Isobel, brushing her long dark hair, and admired her.

Isobel looked down at the table. "I'm sorry about your mother." He could see her in the mirror in front of her, eyes sad. Isobel carried herself strong, but when it came to people she cared for, empathy crushed her.

"To hell with her." Dresden sat up.

Isobel left the vanity, returned to the bed and put her arms around him. "We have each other. You're my lover and my best friend."

Dresden kissed her forehead. "Through thick and thin. . ."

They pulled away, looked into each other's eyes. So much thought conveyed through a single stare. She tugged on his hair and bit her lower lip. He leaned his head back and closed his eyes. Reopened his eyes and pulled up her slip. He searched for her lips with his fingers. Her hands found the buttons to his pants. He rolled her onto her back and bit and kissed her neck and shoulders. Their sounds mixed with the sounds of the television in the background.

"—the correlation between the strange volcanic eruptions, the world's gangrene epidemic, the deterioration of . . . god . . . uh, with us now are two experts in—"

Isobel whispered, "What are we watching?"

"—is the planet hemorrhaging blood? Are the reports—"

Dresden said, "I don't know."

He found the remote and turned it off. Isobel turned his head back toward her and pulled him in for a kiss. Wrapped her legs tightly around him and pressed her face into his neck.

The dead television's speaker crackled.

Ring around the rosie, a pocket full of posies, ashes,
ashes, we all fall down . . .

The rhyme had been faint but Isobel was sure she'd
heard it and then it was gone. And in her periphery, she
thought she'd imagined the face of a man on the screen. But
when she turned to better look the screen was black.

"What's wrong?"

"Nothing." Isobel shrugged. "Kiss me."

IV

Later Dresden woke from a scratching at the window.

Isobel was still asleep. He brushed aside her hair and
kissed the side of her head. The scratching persisted. He rolled
off of the bed, found his pants on the floor and strolled over
to the window where the sound was. He didn't see anything
outside.

He went to the kitchen to get some water, navigating
through the darkness with ease. Stood in front of the sink
and admired the moon through the window. He heard the
way his glass was almost full. Lowered his eyes and was
startled to see a silhouette in the window over the sink. He
jumped back and spilled water everywhere.

He instinctively looked down. "Shit."

Dresden looked back up at the window and the figure
was gone. He got closer to the glass and looked around
outside. Wondered if he had imagined it. Realizing the water
was still running, he turned off the tap and searched the
countertop for a towel to soak up the spill.

His eyes had adjusted by the time he got to the hallway
and noticed the front door was open. He paused and turned
to face the door and stared. *Had the door been like that?*
He hadn't heard anything. He blinked hard, hoping to shake
off imagination. The door remained open and a draft came
in through it. Behind him, at the end of the hall, he could
see Isobel sleeping in bed in their room. He turned back to

the door, saw movement and felt himself get tackled down. Hands at his throat. He couldn't say anything, couldn't yell to warn Isobel. The glass shattered on the floor. All went dark.

V

Birds sang sweetly outside. Isobel yawned and stretched in bed. It felt like every vertebrae in her spine popped. Remnants of the night's dreams danced in her mind: a vintage recording of Ring-Around-the-Rosie, a small, strange man staring at her from the foot of the bed, the color green, bright lights, rotten flesh, screaming. The man at the foot of the bed stuck out—he had strobed in and out of being there, like a scrambled television channel. In spite of the nightmares, Isobel still felt rested and ready for the day ahead.

She reached over for Dresden and felt only the mattress.

"Hmmm."

Isobel shrugged, kicked off the sheets and stood. Something seemed off. She shuffled toward the kitchen, stepped on something sharp and yelped. Picked up her foot and examined it, finding a small shard of glass. She looked down and didn't see anything broken on the floor, assumed it must have been something she'd missed sweeping. Isobel wiped at the small dot of blood and looked around for slippers. Found a pair of his shoes instead and put them on.

"Dresden?" No answer.

Maybe he had slipped out to surprise her with breakfast. He'd done this before and so she decided she'd wait.

Several hours passed and there was still no sign of Dresden. Isobel reheated some old coffee she found in the pot and thought about their situation. They were going to be married—

"Oh no," she whispered to herself. "I hope he didn't get cold feet . . ."

But he wasn't the superstitious kind (he'd already seen her in the dress and fucked her in it) and they both seemed so sure, so in love, there couldn't be any reservation now . . . could there? Isobel chuckled at the thought of being stood up, but then she began to worry. Maybe he was already there at the chapel. It was so close to the time . . .

She changed into the wedding gown, put on her combat boots and left a note in case he had only been held up.

Isobel parked her car and stared up at the Tower of Chapels through the windshield. The building made her feel very small. It might as well have been a skyscraper. Her heart pounded in her chest and her hands clammed up. Isobel closed her eyes and remembered the day Dresden had come with her to reserve the date. They had gone in excitedly holding hands, grinning like shitheads, ear to ear.

Which one, my dear? Dresden said to Isobel.

There are so many options. She looked over the hundreds of chapels listed in the building's directory. Space-themed, 8-bit, under the sea, 80's heist film, slasher movie—all the possibilities for a wedding seemed to exist within the building.

Whoa, an Enter the Dragon *wedding! Dresden struck a kung fu pose. Yellow tracksuits?*

Oh god. Hello Kitty even. Isobel sighed, amused but also slightly annoyed. Ooh, a Vegas Chapel! I wonder what that's like. That's that fake city from the Nicolas Cage movie, right?

I think so, yeah.

Isobel said, I wonder if we can get a Fat Elvis to marry us.

Dresden moved his hips like Elvis and pointed at her. Hell yeah. Let's check it out and if it sucks we can just choose another one. Like the Bruce Lee one.

We're so not having a kung-fu wedding.

Aw man. Dresden slumped his shoulders and gave her puppy dog eyes. She shook her head. He smiled and quickly scooped her up, buried his face in her neck and gnawed at her neck.

Isobel chuckled to herself. Opened her eyes and realized she was here again, alone this time.

"Fat Elvis, here I come," she said.

Isobel got into the elevator and looked at the directory—there were no numbers, only chapel names on the buttons. Who knew which floor the Vegas Chapel was on. Judging from how long it took on the lift, though, it was easy to assume it was at the top. The elevator stopped and went silent. The door opened and a bright light flooded in. Isobel shielded her eyes and stepped into it.

Two
EVERYTHING
IS UGLY

I

Isobel shielded her eyes and stepped out of the elevator. The sky inside was blue, cloudless, and had its own sun. The floors were hardpan, cracked and dusty and crumbling under each step she took. A single tumbleweed rolled past Isobel. The distance held a modest white chapel. A neon road sign protruded from the ground, though there was no road. It read "WELCOME TO VEGAS" and as soon as she'd read it a float of showgirls in very elaborate sequin gowns gracefully strolled out the front doors of the chapel. Music she was sure might be the theme to *Match Game* came on over the chapel's PA and a moment later Elvis shuffled out and waved. It wasn't really Elvis, she knew, just an overweight man with sideburns wearing a white jumpsuit that looked like it'd rip at any moment. His hair and tan looked like they'd been sprayed on.

The Elvis belched and waved. "Thank you, thank you very much." His accent needed work.

He patted around the jumpsuit like he'd forgotten something, had an "a-ha" moment and reached in through the chest opening and down to his crotch and removed a pair of gold Tiger Man sunglasses. He adjusted them and sauntered over to Isobel, who stood there blank and nervous with her arms at her side.

"Uh huh. Where's the rest of your party?" His words slurred.

"On their way?" Isobel shrugged.

Elvis inexplicably vomited and she sidestepped it. He wiped his mouth with his sleeve.

"You've been drinking." Isobel saw no point in subtlety.

"Naw." He retched again, but nothing came out. "Well, a little, sure."

"You're a minister."

"I also do birthdays."

"Great." Her eyes rolled. Isobel had expected Dresden to be here and he wasn't, and now this. Her heart sank in her chest a little. "Just great."

"Let's hope that weddin' party gets here soon 'cause we got places to be. You ain't the only bride in the world." He walked her toward the chapel. Fat Elvis slapped one of the showgirls on the ass as they passed. The showgirl furrowed her brow and her smile wavered, but only briefly—a glimpse of disappointment come and gone in a fraction of a second.

"So, that's it?"

Fat Elvis turned around and scoped the scenery, not finding anything wrong with it. "Were you expecting somethin' else, darlin'?"

"Manners? I'm supposed to be getting married today."

Fat Elvis chuckled. "Ain't no groom, ain't no weddin'."

Isobel crossed her arms and her head slumped. She stared at the ground and contemplated leaving. Dug the toe of her right boot in the ground and fought back crying. Her face reddened and her eyes started to water, but she held it.

Fat Elvis sighed. "Listen, it ain't the end of the world if he don't show."

"The world is actually ending, you know."

"Probably. Who cares? You want a tour of the place while we wait?"

Isobel sniffled. "I . . . sure, okay."

"Tour's real short. There's the sky, there's the sand, that's the chapel . . ." He reached into his jumpsuit again and found a flask. "And this is the whiskey."

21

II

His head throbbed. It felt like thousands of fists trying to punch their way out of his skull. He tried to open his eyes but they felt glued shut.

He groaned. "Isobel . . ."

"Oh good. You're awake," said Elise.

"Where's Isobel?" He couldn't see yet, but he turned his head in the direction of her voice.

"Dresden, my boy, I knew you would be fine."

His eyes slowly opened and he attempted to lift his head off of the pillow. It felt heavy and he let it drop. He heard a rhythmic tone.

"Where are we?" He groaned and tried to focus on the room around him. It looked as sterile as a hospital. He strained to look at a monitor beside him. The tone was his heart, a bouncing dot on the screen.

"You're safe is all you need to know."

"Where is Isobel?" Dresden felt impatient and hot. His headache intensified.

"You're home."

Nothing about the room looked familiar to him and something about her tone was unsettling.

"Home? This isn't your house." He'd been in every room of it since he was a boy, there was no way this was the same place.

Elise nodded her head endearingly. "Yes, dear, we're home."

He remembered getting up for a glass of water and widened his eyes. The silhouette in the window, the open door, the struggle . . . "How long have I been out?"

Elise whispered, "Quiet, rest now." One hand hovered an inch above his forehead and the other hand picked up a bell on the table beside the bed. She rang it twice.

It wasn't long before a person in scrubs and a mask walked into the room. "Ah, the patient is awake. Time for another shot, then."

"Well enough, Doctor." Elise nodded at her.

"What? Shot? What's going on?" Dresden strained to move, but he could only raise his head and his fingers. "Where's Isobel. I'm not asking."

"The kind doctor is going to give you some medicine now. You'll be nice and strong again in no time." Dresden's mother patted his shoulder. Tears welled in her eyes.

"I don't need medicine. I need Isobel. I'm supposed to—"

Elise put on surgical gloves and picked up Dresden's hand and cupped it in hers. Looked him in the eyes and smiled. "Dresden, dear, Isobel didn't make it."

Panic. "W-what?"

"She's dead."

The doctor coughed into her hand and shook her head. Elise arched a brow and shot the doctor a disapproving glance. Dresden was too sedated to catch the exchange. He felt like he'd been hit by a truck. His jaw slacked and he went silent. The skin on his face felt like it was on fire. He wanted to cry and vomit, but he did neither.

"I'm sorry to tell you that."

He stared at the ceiling and said, "Leave me alone."

Elise pursed her lips and let go of his hand. She stood up to leave, but before she left the room, she turned to the doctor and callously said, "Dose him."

The doctor approached and said, "This won't hurt a bit." She stuck him with the hypodermic and cooed. Thumbed down the syringe and cold fluid rushed into Dresden's veins. He didn't flinch or blink. Kept his stare on the ceiling and thought about Isobel. If she were dead, then he hoped to join her. "Good boy." The doctor withdrew the needle and wiped the puncture. Peeled and placed a bandage over it. "Your mother said these were your favorite."

Dresden, feeling very numb, slowly looked down at the Band-Aid box on the surgical tray next to the bed. "Bat . . . " Dresden went under.

He heard soft humming and the sound of metal knitting needles clicking together. His eyes slowly forced themselves open. The pounding in his head had receded. He groaned.

"How are you feeling?" His mother was with him.

"Like shit. What is that doctor giving me?"

"Medicine."

"What kind?"

"The kind that will make you healthy and strong so you can live a very long life." Elise smiled at the yarn she worked in her hands.

Dresden's eyes widened. "You're not dosing me w-with *that* medicine, are you?"

Elise stopped knitting and looked at Dresden. "Of course I am. You're my last child. I'm no longer fertile. The doctor has confirmed this. I need to make sure that you don't die on me like the others have."

Rage boiled up inside of Dresden. "How could you? Did you stop to think that maybe I don't want this medicine?"

"That's why we started dosing you while you were unconscious."

"How a many doses have you given me?"

"A few," Elise said and nonchalantly started knitting again.

"How many?"

Elise bit her lip and furrowed her brow. "Two?"

Dresden glared at her. "How many?"

Elise loudly exhaled. "You've been dosed five times."

Dresden hit the palm of his hand against his forehead. The pounding heightened again. His mother stared. "Dresden . . . you have to trust me."

"I don't." He took deep breaths. "What makes you think I want to live alongside you?"

Elise sat up and tried to hold her composure. "A son should love his mother."

"You're not a mother . . . you're a fucking monster."

"I gave birth to you."

"No you didn't. Science did. I'm a lab experiment. I was practically hatched."

"It was still my egg." Elise shrugged and knitted.

Dresden's blood rushed his skin, temper growing. He almost shouted, but he noticed the lavender gloves. He tried to remember if she had ever touched him, skin to skin. He couldn't think of a time. But these gloves were new, more aesthetic than medical. Red dripped from the base of her palm.

"What's wrong with your hands?"

"Nothing." Elise rolled her eyes.

"Tell me."

"Dresden, I'd really appreciate you not to . . ." Elise trailed. Blood ran down a nostril and she looked winded. She reached up and touched at her philtrum, and looked at the blood on her gloved fingertips. Her expression was one of horror.

Elise inaudibly mouthed something at her hand.

"What is this? Your hands are leaking and now you've got a bloody nose."

"This isn't happening." Elise was speaking to herself, ignoring him now. "Nurse." Her controlled expression fell away to panic. "Nurse!"

The door opened and the nurse came in. "Yes, Mrs. . . . oh my god." The blood flowed freely now from Elise's nose.

"Don't stand there like an idiot," Elise shrieked. "Help!"

Dresden sat up and tried to make sense of the situation unfolding. The nurse called for the doctor and the doctor came running in, carrying a kit that contained syringes and different colored vials. The doctor put on gloves and prepared to dose Elise with light blue medicine.

"What the fuck is going on?"

"Your mother just needs a treatment is all." The doctor injected Elise.

"Don't lie to me. There's something wrong with her hands. Her head too. Why's she bleeding like that?" He trailed off, watching his mother get doped. Found himself feeling sorry for her.

Elise looked back at him, the nurse wiping blood off of her face, and she said, "Don't worry about me, little one. Your momma will be just fine." Elise lifted her hand and it dropped heavily, attempting to wave off his concern.

"We should bandage up these hands, too," the doctor said to the nurse.

The nurse nodded and went to a cabinet for some bandages. The doctor prepped her tool tray and waited. When the nurse returned he began to peel off Elise's gloves. The fabric resisted being pulled from her skin and ripped it. Dresden cringed but couldn't stop watching. Her hands looked charred and cracked, and they oozed pus. The odor hit him and he gagged.

"The hell?"

"No swearing," Elise muttered, medicine-drunk.

Dresden was mortified. "You look sick."

"You have nothing to worry about." Elise raised her brows and chuckled. "People like us don't die. We have the best care." She nodded at the doctor. "The best . . ."

"You've got that . . . the sickness that's all over the news."

"Oh Dresden. Past tense. I *had* the illness." Elise smiled.

"I hope it's not contagious . . ."

"But we caught it before it escalated," she continued. "Same as we've done during all the other epidemics. Darling, we practically engineer these things to keep the lower populace in check. Of course even we're bound to catch it sometime . . ."

"You can't be serious."

"How else do you think I've managed to live all this time?" Elise flinched as the doctor bandaged her. "Two hundred and twenty-three *beautiful* years."

"Your hands weren't like that when I got here. You're still sick."

"Oh hush. The body's just healing its—"

Dresden said, "Your body is going to rot."

"I won't be dead."

"You'll look like a corpse for the rest of your life."

The doctor looked up at him but didn't say anything. Elise huffed.

Dresden said, "A fucking zombie."

"Ha. Honey, a little plastic surgery and I'll be as good as new."

Dresden tried to stand but fell.

"You shouldn't do that," said the doctor. "I'm surprised you can stand."

Dresden stood back up and pulled off nodes and slid the catheter out of his arm. He gripped it in his hand like a knife. The nurse stood and opened his mouth to say something. Dresden shot him a hard look and raised the needle. "Don't." The nurse remained still. Dresden limped over toward Elise and said, "You disgust me." His mother didn't seem to hear. He glanced again at the doctor and the nurse. "Not sure which one of you blindsided me in the dark, but if you wanna try that again . . ." He coughed. Held the needle confidently. "Bye, Elise. Don't come for me this time."

Dresden backed his way to the door, keeping his eyes on the help. His mother didn't look at him.

"You want us to go after him?" asked the nurse.

"No, no," Elise waved a bandaged hand. "He's made his point, but he won't get far. Children never forget where their home is." Dresden stopped in the doorway and stared. "You know what you *can* get for me?"

The doctor said, "Anything."

"Vodka tonic. Perhaps an escort."

Dresden mouthed, "What?" and edged his way out, shutting the door behind him. Horn speakers lined a concrete corridor that looked vaguely military. A sound like a microphone being switched on. He expected an alarm. They crackled but no announcement ever came.

Sitting on the steps of the chapel, Isobel had tucked her dress around her legs so that it looked as though she were wearing a giant diaper. This allowed her to move her legs much more easily without dirtying her dress or letting Fat Elvis catch a glimpse of her underwear. He had already tried. Isobel undid the bun on her head and let her hair fall. Wind lightly blew the mustard dust over her.

Fat Elvis hiccupped. "Yer a good lookin' woman."

Isobel laughed. "I'm getting married." But that hadn't sounded as confident as she'd intended it to. "You're drunk."

He leaned in and whispered. "I ain't that drunk. And ya ain't married yet."

"Yet." Isobel looked at the ground.

"Besides, what if he don't show?" He put his hand on her leg and held it there. His fingers were heavily calloused and tar-stained. Still, he had a point. What if Dresden didn't show? The thought lingered in her head, began its slow drip into her stomach where it became an anxious ball of mass. His hand started to trace up toward her thigh.

She pushed Fat Elvis' hand away gently and mumbled, eyes staring into space, "He has to come. We're in love."

Fat Elvis chuckled, inched closer and place his hand back on her leg, this time further up. The showgirls surrounded them, their expressions conveying a deep vacancy and sadness. Isobel wondered why they were like that. Isobel grabbed one of his fingers and bent it back. Fat Elvis yelped and his fake pompadour shifted on his head, his face contorted with pain.

Isobel said, "Are you going to behave?"

He hesitated; she bent his finger farther back. Fat Elvis yelped louder and nodded vigorously. Isobel let go of his hand and shoved it back at him. The minister held his hand to his chest and whimpered. Isobel looked at the horizon and wondered how they got a sun in here. Turned to the elevator and couldn't see the door anymore. No exit, no sign of Dresden. They were all startled by a distant, steady wheezing somewhere in the desert. The showgirls looked at each other. Isobel looked at Fat Elvis.

"You heard that, right?" she asked.

"Yup." Coughs and groans resonated from the same distance. Fat Elvis looked at the sky and he fidgeted with his sunglasses. All the calm had drained from his orange face. The scenery began to flicker between different backdrops.

"Holograms," Isobel whispered.

The wheeze was a similar sound to the one a tube television makes when it's switched off. The showgirls, Fat Elvis and Isobel glanced around a large room they now found themselves in. It looked like an inversion of a Lemarchand's box. The ground pulsed and began to shake violently.

Isobel fell over and rolled with the moving church. *The floor's metal*, she realized. It looked like steely flesh, translucent, stretched over rebar that was networked just beneath the surface, like veins. Isobel crawled off of the church's porch and reached to touch the ground, expecting it to feel like rubber or maybe steel. Her hand went straight through like it was tissue paper. There was a loud pop, like an instance of a sonic boom. The room began to deflate, whistling as air left it. The showgirls screamed and Isobel felt movement, almost as if the room were drifting. Felt herself getting pulled toward the hole she had torn. Isobel reached for the wood of the church's deck but found nothing.

Wind violently rushed in and threw the showgirls and Fat Elvis into the air. The showgirls screamed, flailing, their sequins and feathers were like rainbows forming over the industrial backdrop of the collapsing bubble. Fat Elvis seemed like he were trying to swim through the air. He vomited.

Isobel was jerked through the hole by an expulsion of air and she plummeted through charred metal and landed somewhere flat on her back. Pain shot through her body. Isobel gasped and tried to get up but could only move her arms. She tried to call out and couldn't. Isobel coughed and all sound was drowned out by a loud cracking. She scanned her surroundings, what turned out to be another room like the one she'd just been expelled from, and she saw more pieces of the ceiling she'd come through breaking off and falling all around her. Metal and rebar bent and seemed poised to fall onto her. It gave under its weight and she threw up her arms to shield her head.

Three
NO ONE IS SAFE

I

Her vision hazy, Isobel tried to piece together what had just happened. This room had not deflated like the last; it seemed more solid. The ceiling's rupture seemed to have stopped breaking apart for the moment.

"Dresden," she said, weakly.

Her sight focused and she strained to sit up. The hurt kept her down. This room looked burnt at the edges, but otherwise the same as when the Vegas Chapel had shorted out. Isobel listened. What had happened to Dresden?

"Whatever happened," she whispered, "I hope you're safe."

Isobel managed to raise her head and could see the rubble that covered her legs. Her arms were caked with blood and dirt. She brushed concrete dust off of herself. There were boulder-sized chunks with jagged metal sticking out of them all around her. Isobel groaned and bit her lip hard enough to taste blood. Tried to clear away the rubble as best she could so she could see what she was trapped under. She gasped when she saw the spear of rebar that had pierced her calf through the shin, looking like it'd just slighted the bone by less than an inch. The metal was bent too, holding up the weight of the debris it was attached to. Had it not been there, she was sure, her legs would have been crushed. But she was still trapped.

The wound didn't look fresh. Blood had caked, crusted around the bar. Rather, it looked as if it had healed already with the rebar still inside, skin starting to grow over the metal. Isobel tried to move the leg and pain jolted hot through her leg. She grimaced and held still until it subsided. Sweat mudded the dust on her face. The wound started to bleed. She tried again and screamed. Let herself fall back and lay still. Started to cry.

The building groaned and she sat up, listening, held her sobbing back. Isobel searched for the sound's origin. The walls pulsed around here and they seemed to take on that seem "living" appearance as the Vegas Chapel had before it'd collapsed. She wondered if the showgirls and Fat Elvis were dead, crushed. *Probably*, she thought. Like the Vegas Chapel there was no exit door to be found in here. But there was a window. It had to be safer than waiting for the same thing to happen again. How could she get to it?

Isobel looked down at the bar, clear through her leg. The wheezing got louder and she panicked. Took a deep breath and held it. Reached for the rebar and gripped it tight. Isobel pulled, wishing like hell she didn't have to do it. The wound tore open a little and blood spurted out, but the leg stayed firmly in place.

The room shook. Isobel reached around and found a jagged rock of concrete and picked it up. Tried to ignore the dizziness. Told herself she wanted to see Dresden again more than anything in the world. She reached her into her dress's cleavage and found her car keys. Bit down on a rubber keychain in the shape of a cat.

Isobel struck the edge of her leg with the rock and whimpered. Struck it again and almost blacked out, vision going all spotty, but she kept awake. She struck the leg until it tore loose of the metal. Her teeth bit hard into the keychain. The meat was stubborn, but then it gave with a rip. Her body surged alive with adrenaline. Her eyes scanned blood on the rock, blood soaked up the dress. Isobel was free.

She dropped the rock and tried to stand. Fell and caught herself on the debris. Another tremor struck the room again and her vision tightened. The blood came generous and she tore herself a tourniquet from a strip of the dress and tied it above the wound. She needed to get out. She needed to stay alive. Isobel hobbled to the window and looked out and saw how high up she was. Only a few stories. Realized she'd be down there either with the building or without it soon enough.

The tremor grew and it felt as though the whole building were shaking. A shadow washed over her. She looked up and saw a body fall from the sky. Her eyes followed it down and saw it flop onto a pile of bodies. It remained there motionless. So many bodies were out there. Other people who'd jumped or maybe fallen. *There're so many of them*, she thought. *How many rooms did the building have?* The directory had seemed infinite. Now all these people were dead. She shook her head and tried to focus. Isobel stepped back, the leg numb for the moment, but a noticeable lack of mobility now. *Maybe I'll have better luck?* She hobbled forward, throwing all her weight out in front of her and leapt through the glass, exploding it. She pirouetted down in a torrent of shards.

The fall came and went too quickly for her to comprehend it. Her body landed on the pile of bodies and debris. The smell was insufferable. They didn't look newly dead, looked like they were in a state of decomposition. Had they been there a while? Had *she* been there a while? The wind carried in the scent of fucked-up barbecue. *It's the disease*, she thought. *What if I've got it too?*

There was something else. The angle of her shredded leg looked strange. She'd landed on it wrong. Her leg was broken now.

"Oh g—" There was a thunderclap up in the sky. Isobel looked and saw smoke and fire pouring out of the Tower of Chapels. Figures erupted from windows farther above and landed messily around her, bodies crushed on impact and decomposing. Smoke clouded around the top of the building and it began to implode, an upside down mushroom cloud of dust and ash coming down on her.

Isobel crawled over the bodies and hit pavement. The tower quaked and the dust cloud came before the rest of the building did. Such destruction, the fall of a leviathan. She put her weight on her good leg and hobbled as quickly as she could toward her car. Patted herself for the keys but realized they were still in the building. Checked the door and saw she'd left it unlocked. She opened the door and climbed into the backseat. Door locked, she huddled there a while. The wave of dust overtook the car and rocked it, misting the air, a blizzard. The building disintegrated to nothing and she passed out.

It didn't last long though. Isobel woke to stillness and the throbbing of her broken leg. She tried to remember everything that had happened. She had come to the Tower of Chapels because she and Dresden were getting married. But . . .

The Chapel. Dresden.

Wait. Yes. She remembered now. Her wedding dress was tattered and dirty, the lower half of it stained red. She'd loved that dress. Dresden was still heavy on her mind and she hoped he was okay. Hoped he had no-showed after all so that he wouldn't have been in the structure when it came down.

Isobel felt cold suddenly. Thought it might be the leg. She found an old hoodie on the floorboard and put it on over the dress, zipped it up. That helped some. Outside looked toxic. She found a bandana of Dresden's in the armrest's console and an unopened bottle of water that looked like it'd been under the seat for some time. Isobel uncapped it and drank, just then understanding how thirsty she was. Water quickly absorbed into her body, helping her feel like a new person. After she finished the bottle she tied the bandana over her nose and mouth and pulled up the hood. Everything else in the car was just pillows, CDs, books and a magazine, art supplies. Nothing she'd take with her. Isobel looked through the window and looked at her leg. Bone jutting out. But the bleeding from the torn muscle had slowed, the tourniquet doing its job. There was no one else around as far as she could see. Just the bodies and the rubble. She'd have to reset the bone and make a splint and then find a payphone and try and call for help. Isobel reached for the door handle and stopped when the radio came on.

"What the fuck?" She looked at the empty ignition.

The frequency's digital display read 76.5 and it staticked. Faintly she heard the same nursery rhyme she'd heard at home and she immediately felt sick. Children laughing. The radio crackled and went quiet. She wondered if maybe she'd gone crazy. *Deal with your head later.*

Isobel opened the car door and emerged into the mist.

She squinted, trying to look for something to use as a splint. Tried to remember how she'd seen it done on television. Shove the bone back in place, tie some wood to it, something like that. Isobel scanned around. Saw a short length of broken rebar on the ground but nothing to match it. Hobbled over to where there were bodies and thought she'd look for something there. What was the harm if she was already infected? But the bodies had already decomposed beyond what she'd seen earlier. Isobel felt that same sick feeling she'd got when the radio came on in the car. Something was wrong here, not just this day, but with the world . . . the building had come down, but where were the news crews? And the police? Fire trucks, anything? *Help's not coming,* she looked down to the ground. *Jesus I'm all alone here.* The mist was still settling but it seemed as if there was less of everything than there had been. Like some of the building had outright evaporated. Isobel dry heaved when she saw a body that seemed as if its skin had melted right off of the bone. Looked at the rebar in her hand and made a connection. Knew what she needed to do. She scraped the remaining flesh off of the body's left leg with the rebar and pulled on the femur. It came off much easier than she'd expected, tore right out from the rotten muscle and tendons.

"And now the bad part."

Isobel lowered slowly to a seated position on the pavement and decided to try to push in the bone and wrap her leg. She applied pressure and it wouldn't budge. The bad leg looked a little shorter than the good leg and she realized this would be harder than she wanted it to be. The leg was mostly numb but she knew if she started to mess with it the pain would get bad quick. Isobel tried to think.

"I need to stretch it out and . . ."

Two large chunks of concrete nearby had landed close together in the building's fall. The sides of them came to touch in a tight V shape. It was a bad idea, she knew, but couldn't think of other options. Isobel pulled herself back up, keeping the weight off of the broken leg and hobbled over. She tore more of her dress and wrapped lightly it around the protruding bone in a loop and held onto the end. She lifted her leg slowly to where her boot sat snug in the nook of the two concrete forms.

"You can do this," she attempted to motivate herself.

Isobel leaned away with all her weight, feeling her leg stretch slightly. She pulled on the loop she'd made and tightened it, and the bone slowly, painful started to move back in. Isobel wrapped it around her fist and elbow and pulled tighter, screamed and her vision went spots and she fainted again.

II

Loud masticating sounds. Her entire body hot with sweat. Broken, jagged consciousness. Something soft landed on her face, wet, a scent like tin. *Meat?* Isobel's eyes shot open and she tried to stand but her leg was still caught in the nook. She coughed through the bandana and swatted the piece of meat off of her face. She raised herself up and freed her leg. Kept the weight off of it and looked up and saw the silhouette of a person in the mist, standing over debris. It moved closer and she noticed its skin, rotted and burnt, covered in boils. The boils looked picked at. She opened her mouth to gasp and the figure drew closer to her and released a high-pitched shriek. Spit, blood, and bile sprayed out of its mouth along with the most putrid case of halitosis.

Isobel turned to run and slipped onto more of the bodies.

She struggled to get back up. A hand came up from under the corpses and took her by the arm. Isobel screamed and the other creature loomed closer. She tried to jerk free and the arm holding her tore free, bleeding freely. Isobel stood up and raised the arm like a bat. The creature was humanoid, dressed in dirty, tattered clothes that looked like they'd been expensive, once. It came at her and she swung and knocked it off balance. The creature fell, spit broken teeth, hissed. It started to get up and she hit it again, the meaty part of the arm falling apart in her hands. Isobel screamed at it, tired, unloading everything.

"You." Isobel turned the arm over, its hand aimed like the end of a spear. "Die." The creature hissed again and she shoved the severed arm into its mouth, fist first. Pushed down harder and the jaw and throat gave and the arm went until it stopped. "Now." The creature gagged, foaming around its lips and the arm. "Okay?"

Isobel hit the severed arm's humerus with her palm and broke it. Pulled the sharp end out of the meat of the brachium and stabbed the creature with it. Isobel screamed, almost primitive in her action. She stuck it repeatedly until it stopped moving, and she left the bone spiked in its chest. Isobel fell forward onto the body and cried into her hands. The body twitched beneath her, dead. She pushed herself up and looked at where the arm had come up and grabbed her. Movement, but whatever was under there was trapped under the weight. Isobel left it and crawled over the where she'd reset her leg and fixed the splint, the femur and strip of rebar, and she tied them around the break. Put some weight on her leg and headed toward the road where there had to be a payphone.

III

Isobel found the phone booth across the street. When she picked up the receiver, it crumbled in her hand. She stared at the plastic crumbs as they cascaded down her arm, confused. Turned back to look at the way she'd come. Where the Tower of Chapel's had been there was only ruins that were crumbling, breaking down to smaller pieces.

"How?"

Isobel thought of the way the bodies had rotted so quickly, how the building had come apart around her. Nothing was safe anymore, was it? If she was infected, it wouldn't take long till she was gone too. One thing was certain, she felt. Isobel had to find Dresden before it all went to waste.

Four
THE WORLD
IS DYING

I

Dresden wandered the long corridor. He felt better. Like he had energy again, like whatever tranquilizers they'd pumped him with had burned through. He had never been in this part of his mother's house before. The hall stretched hundreds of feet, dozens of doors along it that all looked the same and led to more rooms or halls, like an underground labyrinth. He didn't know which way he'd come anymore and he had no idea where he even was. Dresden kept walking and hoped it wasn't as big as it seemed.

Was this really his mother's house?—the same house he'd grown up in?

He tried a door and followed the hall behind it. This hall was less industrial, finished more like a hotel with dull, neutral colors and tight looped carpet.

"Like Snoopy's fucking doghouse," he said under his breath.

Dresden opened another door and saw a lounge with a chaise and a window.

"Promising."

The window looked out into a garden. A butterfly flew past the window and he smiled at it, thinking he was close. There were two other doors on each end of the room, to the sides of the one he'd come in from. The door to his right was locked. He tried the other door and it opened into another room that looked identical to the one he was just in. He shrugged and tried the next one and they ran the same

39

route he assumed the hall would have. He walked for an hour. Dresden finally decided to backtrack and found the door he'd just come in was locked. He glanced back out the window and saw that the butterfly had come to rest on the window. He walked through the unlocked door and found the same view. Different room, but the same décor and the butterfly was there. He ran to the next door, held it open and looked into both rooms.

The butterfly existed in two places at once.

". . . huh?"

He sank to his knees, defeated. The room felt like it was spinning around him. This maze, his mother, Isobel . . . Isobel, was she alive? Dead? Her eyes . . . He blinked hard and shook his head. Lips, smile. His eyes welled and he balled his hands into fists. Breasts, hips, skin. The way she laughed and smelled. His brain felt like it'd opened floodgates. His head burned. He threw his arms out and yawped.

Dresden walked into the new room and the door shut behind him. He went to the corner, took a lamp off of a chair side table and threw it at the wall. He picked up the chair side table and ran at the window and struck it. The window flickered, but didn't shatter--a shatterproof monitor. He turned and flung the small table across the room. It went right through the colonial painting beside the unlocked door. It clattered into a dark space. Dresden relaxed his anger and ran to the hole and looked in.

Another room, not this same one.

He scratched the back of his head. "Interesting."

Dresden tore more of the canvas and climbed out through the wall, and into the new room.

II

Her leg felt worse, but when she'd searched for the police station it was ruin. The few squad cars she'd passed had rusted, their tires dried and broken, skeletons in the seats.

There was no sign there'd even been a hospital, aside from the foundation and fine dust she knew had once been the building, the equipment . . . people. Home was still far away and she didn't think she'd make it there that night. Isobel limped to where some rusted vehicles were parked and figured there was no telling what, if anything, would be left when she woke. If she would even wake up again. She was too exhausted to care and laid down in the grass. *At least there's still that.* The grass was comfortable. She whispered a goodbye to Dresden just in case and closed her eyes.

Morning did come and she woke to a strange sucking sound. She squinted her eyes, remembering immediately the day before when she'd come to and seen the creature over her, eating the remains of the dead. Isobel squinted her eyes and perked her head up, looking around.

"Oh hell," she said. The head at her feet was bald, thin red hairs still clinging at the sides. Skin stretched tight over the skull. It looked up at her, vaguely female. This creature's nasal cavity was mostly visible, the nose having rotted off fairly recently. Blood caked its underbite. Thick strands of saliva leaked from its mouth. The creature had been biting the boot of Isobel's splinted leg, but its teeth were mostly black gums. Isobel was frozen, watching it go back to tonguing the leather.

Isobel kicked wildly at it with her good side and heard a crack. She pulled her leg back and saw she'd knocked its jaw off. The creature was dressed in floral print sundress that might have been beautiful if not for the gore. It looked down at its jaw, confused. Isobel felt almost sad for it, but then the look degenerated into anger. It raised up, gurgling at her, its tongue bobbing snakelike.

"Uh . . ."

Isobel scooted back as the creature stood. There was no way she'd get up in time. It lumbered forward and fell on her. She put her arm up to its neck, holding it up, keeping its few teeth from gnawing at her. Its tongue licked at her face and she felt herself heave, but nothing came out. Isobel tried to pull its head back by the hair, but her free hand got only a clump of it and a layer of dead skin. The creature's hand found her eye and started to gouge. Isobel grunted, tugged on the rebar in her splint and pulled it free, pain surging up her leg. She brought up the rod and shoved it up through the exposed roof of its mouth, up into its brain. The creature went still immediately and dropped all its weight. Isobel rolled it off of her, pulled out the rod and wiped it off on its sun dress. She got to her feet and tightened the splint, hoping the bone tied to her leg would be able to support her on its own. She turned to look back on what she'd done and vomited, but nothing much came out.

The radios in all of the rusted vehicles came on at the same time.

Ring around the rosie
Pocket full of posies . . .

Isobel hit her palm against her head. "Not this again." There was movement from the corner of her eye. She turned. "Shit." More of them. "Shit." Plural. Isobel had been lucky so far. She didn't plan to test that luck. She limped as fast as she could in the opposite direction.

Grey skies swirled overhead. It looked ready to storm, but it didn't. Hours passed and she hadn't seen much of anything except the ruins of places she once knew. It seemed like an entirely different world than the one she'd gone to bed in just two days before. It smelled awful, though, the rot. She wondered who else had made it. And who hadn't. What if Dresden had decayed out of existence? She'd have nothing. She couldn't think about that. She didn't want to think about that. She had to keep moving. Had to hope she'd find help before an infection set in. Hoped she'd at least stay alive long enough to get infected.

"Bad things seem like good things and that's how you know."

Know what?

"It's so fucking over."

Stop talking to yourself.

What few structures were still standing looked abandoned and dark. The only signs of life were rats, which she unreasonably hated, but she still welcomed them more than most everything else she'd seen thus far.

"We're the survivors, guys," she said to no one, or maybe the rats, who didn't understand anyways.

It struck her suddenly that she might be alone here. The last normal person.

Normal.

"Ha."

Sign posts stood, rusted, but signs with the names of the streets they signified had crumbled into flakes of rust in the broken sidewalks. Basements or foundations, or imprinted dirt in the vague shape of a building that once stood there. *The dirt's already rot . . .*

But had this really been home once? It seemed so alien now.

There was nothing to follow but the vague image of the way things had been. It took imagination and gut instinct, but she found the complex. It had once been a nice building with a well-maintained vintage aesthetic. It still stood, but it looked like it'd been abandoned for decades. Ready to fall any moment. Its fence had crumbled and gave way to a cracked terrace, an uneven gravel path. The bottom floor that had a sign that read, "Office" looked like it'd been bombed out. The paint on the walls was scorched. Isobel imagined an invisible fire all around them, something cosmic that burnt slow. The windows looked bloodshot and the walls quivered. But she wondered if she were imagining that. There wasn't much that seemed real now.

Just like the tower, she remembered. Its rooms, the chapel . . .

Isobel stepped onto the terrace and heard a metallic echo. Looked around, startled. She saw a fisherman's hat poking up from behind a nearby car. He rose and called to her in a loud whisper, "Hey, hey! You don't want to go in there. That building's going to collapse."

"That's my home," Isobel said, pointing at the building.

"Quiet," the man waved his hand downward. He crouched and moved closer to her. "There are . . . *things* all around this area. They'll hear you."

"Oh," she said. "I can handle myself." That felt like a lie.

"Your leg . . ."

"It's fine. I'm fine." Also a lie.

"Listen, there're some of us that are still okay. Immune maybe, or it's just taking longer. I'm a scout for the group. If you want to stay alive . . ."

"I need to get some things."

"Lady, I don't mean to be brief, but you'll die in there."

"Maybe. I'll take my chances." Isobel winked and limped hurriedly into the building, clutching the rebar like a club. The hallways throbbed, almost responding to her steps. The walls looked different, darker. Deep red where they'd once been a light brown, almost the color of eggshells. The red was beautiful.

"Hurry," she told herself. "That guy wasn't wrong." Isobel wondered at what point she'd started talking to herself.

The apartment numbers passed by as she moved quickly. The splint seemed to be holding up and though she'd never get used to the twinge of pain that shot up her leg every time she moved on it, she'd come to expect it now, ceased to feel shocked when it did. Five . . . six . . .

"There."

The last apartment.

She checked the door; it was locked. Her keys had been lost in the tower. Dresden didn't usually lock the door when he was around. It was a habit of his growing up in one of those gated communities, the kind the super affluent had. Security forces along the perimeters, perfect lawns, a veritable utopia. No one got robbed there. And he'd taken that part of his culture with him, though she'd picked on him about it, explained that he couldn't do it. That he'd eventually regret it. It'd never come to that, thankfully, but here it was proof that he wasn't home. She missed even the naïve parts of him. Isobel stepped back and jumped at the door. It didn't give much. She tried again and it broke free, the wood edged with dry rot. Isobel knew what this meant. The collapse would happen soon.

Isobel looked inside. The power didn't work but the sunlight still made it easy enough to see. The walls looked clear and she could see the wiring and pipes, studs and beams, the insulation. It all pulsed, like there was a heartbeat to it. The walls grew darker each beat.

" . . . are ya someone's bride? I can't—"

Isobel gasped, caught off guard. The man in the fisherman's cap stood in the doorway.

"What are you doing here? I thought you would've gone back to your group."

He smiled timidly and shrugged. "Oh, I thought about it. But you left without a goodbye, I figured, hey, maybe she won't want to die alone in there. It's only a matter of time for all of us, ya know."

Isobel laughed. The man was older than her, maybe old enough to be her father. Under the cap, thick tufts of gray hair messily stuck out. His eyes seem kind, she thought. Isobel imagined he was someone's grandfather or husband, he wore a ring, and if he was here alone, maybe he'd also lost . . .

She lowered her head.

"Won't hurt to postpone death a little longer, then. I'll be quick."

Isobel searched around and couldn't find it. No, she worried, it can't be lost. She knocked over a vase, books, digging for it. They'd been rearranging the apartment, didn't know how much longer they'd be in it. But they'd wanted it to feel new for after the wedding. The building shook and they ceiling cracked. Felt like an earthquake.

"Oh, dear," the man sounded worried.

The exterior wall started to buckle. Plaster and cement crumbs littered the floor. Her eyes darted around and she almost gave up. Then she spotted it beneath a stack of art magazines. They must have placed it there when—

The man put his hand on Isobel's shoulder. "We should go."

"Yeah. Right there with you."

She grabbed the picture frame and they hurried out of the apartment. The man slowed his pace for her, committed to what he'd said. The hall's ceiling cracked and buckled. Behind them, some of the ceiling was already giving. It fell and sent dust all the way down the corridor. They coughed hard, but kept moving. The exit wasn't far now, everything getting brighter as they approached sunlight. Thunder as loud as what she'd experienced in the tower shocked through the complex.

Isobel said, "It's coming down."

The man shoved her through the door and the building collapsed. Isobel landed badly and yelped from the jolt of broken bones colliding in her leg. The splint had held. But goddamn, she thought. She remembered the older man and looked around. He'd made it, just barely, caught beneath a small amount of debris. He'd been luckier than she'd been.

"I'm okay," he laughed. "I'm okay."

Isobel nodded. "Thank you. Isobel, by the way."

He said, "Pete. So what was so important?"

"This." She held up the framed picture. "It's my fiancé and I."

"Is he . . . ?"

"Dead? I don't know. He never showed to the wedding."

"Then maybe he's still out there."

"Maybe."

The photograph was of the night they got engaged. Dresden proposing, her expression shocked and excited. Isobel smashed the frame against the road and pulled out the print. Tucked it into her boot and exhaled, relieved.

"If you get to the mini mart on Jefferson and 3rd, you'll find other survivors there." Pete's smile wavered, unable to mask the pain he was in. Isobel walked over to Pete and saw that his arm and leg pinned under concrete. "I'll be fine," he said.

"Bullshit," said Isobel, remembering how alone she'd felt in the Tower of Chapels. Isobel cleared rubble. Pete tried to wave her off. Isobel strained to lift a heavy rock off of his leg. "I'm not leaving without you."

He groaned and tried to move once some of the weight was off. She uncovered his right arm and saw it was trapped beneath a bigger rock at the elbow. It was bent the wrong way.

Isobel said, "Can you move your legs?"

"I think so." Pete looked at his arm. "But," he grimaced, "that . . ."

"Stay with me," said Isobel, seeing that he wanted to sleep.

Pete looked up at her, all that confidence he'd shown earlier fading away. Her heart sank. Isobel hobbled over to a broken two-by-four plank that was under some rubble, freed it and used it as leverage against the weight of the concrete pinning him down. Pried it up slightly and he wrenched his arm free. Blood stained his sleeves. The wood plank snapped and the concrete fell back into place.

Isobel said, "Let me take a look at that."

Pete said, "We've got people at the camp." He shut his eyes a moment. "We better," he coughed, "get going . . . all the noise might have attracted . . ." He trailed but she got the point.

They were both limping now. His broken arm hung uselessly at his side, bleeding down his hands, fingertips, spotting the road as they walked. His back seemed to have taken a beating as well. Isobel had her arm around him, under his shoulder, and they supported each other. The streets looked empty. The still erect buildings were in shambles. Newspapers and trash blew across the street like tumbleweeds. The mini market wasn't far now, but she felt herself growing tired, winded. The sun would be down soon and the power had been out a while now. She hoped they'd make it before it got dark.

They passed a pawn shop that was still somewhat intact, parts of the roof and wall either collapsed in or entirely disintegrated. Its window's glass webbed, the barred door chained and padlocked. Old televisions, typewriters, furniture.

"I wonder if there's anything we could use as a weapon in there," said Isobel.

"It's all been looted," Pete muttered. "Back at the camp . . ."

"If you need a break," she started.

"No, let's keep going."

One of the old televisions blipped on. Green hued images of twin girls playing, static, flower petals, a man's face. . . .

"Are you seeing this?"

Pete said, eyes wide, "I am."

Isobel thought, *Ashes, ashes . . .*

The man blinked and the screen went dead.

Behind them, scrapes and shuffling sounds. Isobel turned and saw more of the creatures.

Pete said "Come on."

They quickened their pace, ignoring the mutual pain and fatigue. Up ahead there was a gas station and a mini mart. She focused on it, said, "Look, that's it, right?"

"Not far now."

Pete fell. Isobel went down with him.

"Pete?"

"I . . ." He fainted.

The creatures closed in. She counted a dozen of them, at least. He'd seemed so afraid of them in numbers and she'd only handled one at a time. Isobel stood up, clutching the metal rod in her hand. Pete hadn't left her and she wasn't about to leave him. She prepared to fight.

Isobel swung with her weight into the head of one of the creatures. It went down, but started to crawl at her. She backed toward Pete's unconscious body and swung the rebar at them, futile attempts to sway them. Isobel took a deep breath and prepared herself to go down fighting. Closed her eyes a second and tensed. Opened them and jutted her body forward to swing and stopped at the sound. In front of her, a creature's eye exploded and it went down. More gunshots. Others popped blood from chests, arms, necks. Fell. Soon it was just her and Pete again, and behind them, footsteps. She turned and saw a mustached man in a sheriff's hat and aviators. A toothpick dangled from chapped lips.

"Who the fuck are you?" the sheriff said to Isobel.

She was too surprised to respond.

More survivors emerged from the doors of the mini mart: a middle-aged woman in a ragged sun dress, a young man in jeans and a blue shirt, an older man dressed like a cowboy with a pooch gut.

They scurried over to Pete and helped carry him inside of the gas station's mini mart.

Isobel held her gaze on the sheriff. "My name's Isobel."

"The fuck kinda name's that?" He spit. Eyed her up and down, eyes fixated on her breasts. Already she disliked him. Her left hand balled into a fist.

"Mack," someone said, from the door of the mini mart. "I think she's with Pete. He's regained consciousness."

The sheriff groaned and cracked his neck. "All right." He bowed slightly, waved his hand toward the building. "After you." The sarcasm she sensed churned her stomach.

Inside the gas station's store, Isobel saw fear. Two children that looked like twins cowered in the corner, a teenage girl in cut-off shorts, her pink hoodie as stained as her own wedding dress. More lost faces. The group that'd helped bring in Pete. He looked defeated, propped up against the wall. The sheriff came up behind her a little too close, breathing hot.

Pete grimaced as someone checked him out. "Isobel . . ."

Isobel watched the lady in the sundress cut his shirt sleeve away. It had looked bad, but when the fabric came free, she realized he was infected. The meat of the arm eaten away from gangrene, the broken bone visible, crumbling. It had that sick sweet smell of dead things.

She said, "How?" But she already suspected.

Pete shrugged and sighed.

Mack said, "There's no how about it. We're all infected, lady."

Isobel's heart sank.

Pete said, "At least I won't become one of those . . ."

"How do you mean?"

Mack said, "Ha, ha, you really don't know. That's a hoot."

"I don't see the joke here."

Pete said, "Don't mind Mack, he's just a bit rough around the edges. He's there where it counts."

Mack said, "They're the one-percenters."

Isobel thought, Dresden comes from . . .

"Rich people always got a cure for everything. Except," he hocked and spit, "this time their little 'vaccine' made it worse, accelerated the deterioration. Made 'em all crazier than a shit house rat, too."

Pete coughed blood and the woman in the sun dress wiped at his mouth.

Isobel said, "And the buildings, cars?"

"We don't think it's a conventional disease," Pete muttered.

Mack said, "Whatever the hell it is, the whole planet's got it."

The woman in the sun dress said, "Let's take a look at that leg."

III

Dresden had wandered into another corridor, this one darker, brick and mortar walls. His eyes struggled to adjust. He navigated the walls, hands grazing slimy old brick. He could hear water dripping somewhere. Rats scurrying. Heavy mildew smell. But he pressed on because he'd seen what waited the other way. He clapped his hands at the rodents to scare them off. The lights came on all at once.

Dresden muttered "Gah," and covered his eyes, blinded.

He thought, *Clapper? Seriously?* His mother so casual in her psychosis.

The hall lit up in bursts and he saw it opened into a larger space filled with aquariums and jars on display podiums, and the brick gave way to a cleaner, almost Victorian finish. He looked around the room. All the containers were full of liquid; inside floated different sized bodies, some still fetal, some deformed, others full grown, otherwise normal. Dark stained wooden shelves. Displays all labeled with names. No rhyme or reason to the organization. He came to the empty aquarium, one of the larger ones and felt sick. He fell to his knees and puked. He looked up again in disbelief. His name on the label.

Epiphany struck him, left him winded: these were his brothers and sisters. His mother had preserved them, all of them. Would preserve him when the time came.

"It's like a trophy room," he said. "I can't believe this."

The body in the aquarium below his opened its eyes. Dresden jumped back, knocked into a podium and fell. The large glass container that was on it shattered and water rushed out, the body of a deformed girl slid across the floor. She opened her eyes, but was otherwise still. He got back on his feet and looked around. All of them staring.

He said, "What do you want from me?"

They blinked, almost in unison.

He looked down at the deformed girl and felt sad. Felt understood. All of them in this room had once understood the hell that is Mother. He took off his hospital gown and wrapped the girl in it. It didn't matter that he was now naked. Dresden held her like a newborn and carried her to the corner of the room and set her sitting up. She gurgled and drooled. It's not fair, he thought. He looked at the name on the podium.

"So your name's Beatriz," he said.

The deformed girl didn't respond to the sound of her own name.

He said, "Yeah, I know the feeling."

Her deformation wasn't subtle in the least. Her eyes weren't centered; one bulged up and out of the socket, more central, almost the dominant feature of a cyclopean face. Two nasal holes in the shape of teardrops that came together briefly only to open out again into a cleft lip. When he'd picked her up, she'd been unexpectedly light. She wasn't very tall, no taller than an infant, but fully matured. He knew she'd have been an adult.

Dresden said, "Were you always like this?"

Beatriz blinked slightly out of sync.

"Sorry for breaking your home." The glass cylinder was in pieces on the floor, the mahogany podium on its side. "This was my home once. I mean not this basement or whatever we're in, but the upstairs, or wherever the actual house is. Had an okay room, I guess. Mother didn't like it when I moved out."

His sister's cyclopean eye looked down. He couldn't read if she understood.

"I've got this nice girl I've been seeing. I don't know, maybe you'd like her. Her name's Isobel."

Beatriz gurgled, spat.

"No, I don't call her 'Bell' or 'Iz,' 'Izzy,' she hates that kind of stuff. I wrote a poem for her and she's like my best friend. I guess she's not just someone I'm seeing, not like a girlfriend—we were supposed to get married. Mother didn't like that. Go figure. When does Elise ever like anything? I mean, you know. You grew up with her, too."

The cyclopean eye focused on him, the pupil expanding and contracting in size.

"She drinks a lot now, if you're wondering. Vodka tonics. Always a fucking vodka tonic. Do you remember that cranberry green tea she used to make *us* drink? Wait, did she make you drink that?" He laughed, darkly. "So bad. It tasted like potpourri or maybe Sears."

Her nose ran. It seemed like every part of Beatriz leaked. Her breathing was heavy and asthmatic.

"How long have you been here?"

The cyclopean eye looked into his, moved its focus toward one of the aquariums. The label with the name, he'd missed the smaller print. He checked the date and did the math. She'd had that brother when she was fourteen. Stood and checked one of the fetuses. Seventy-five years ago. Checked some of the others and couldn't handle it. He leaned down and stared in Beatriz's eyes. She let out a sound like a vague "moo." There were so many years here.

"Enough," he said.

Dresden picked up the cylinder that held the fetus off of its podium and threw it into one of the aquariums. The glass shattered and the water rushed out, washing the bodies out with it. The older woman twitched on the floor. He picked up the podium by its base and swung it into another aquarium, freeing its body. His feet slapped against the wet floor. He went display to display, bashing them in. Glass and water everywhere. He cut his feet on the shards but ignored the sting, blood trailing behind him as he continued to free his siblings. Bodies twitched and mooed and gurgled and spit. But Dresden felt calm, a real calm for the first time in days. He raised the podium over a brother named Burgess and brought it down over his head, caving it. Blood mixed in with the water, swirling. He turned his attention to Siamese twin sisters, Susanne and Kinsley. He did not regret learning their names. Dresden mouthed he was sorry and did it again.

When he'd done enough and there was only him and Beatriz left, Dresden approached her and nodded down out of respect. He closed his eyes, took a deep breath and said, "Trust me, it's better this way." He bashed in the top of her skull. The cyclopean eye rolled up, all white, but the normal eye kept its gaze on him. Dresden let go of the broken podium. The water was red now. He turned to the empty aquarium that'd been meant for him, his own empty future and saw his reflection, nude and spattered with gore. He put his hand on it, spread his fingers. He imagined Isobel on the other side, trapped. He pictured her drowning and knew that somehow he had to help her. But she wasn't behind any glass. It was him in the display and her on the outside somewhere, waiting.

He found a place to sit against the wall. Dresden looked around at what he'd done and understood it as a cold mercy.

He clapped and the lights went out. Dresden wondered what Isobel would think of him now, and he whispered, "Goodnight, my love," not knowing if it was night, but it seemed like it should be. It felt better there in the dark, shivering.

IV

Isobel traced her fingertips over the photo she had tucked into her boot.

"Goodnight, my love," she whispered into the night air.

Five
MEMORIES

They'd met at a punk show in a seedier part of downtown. Dresden would go there discreetly, to lose himself in the music, forget about everything else going on in his life. His first experience in the pit had left his body bruised and sore, and yet he'd come again and again, letting others dole out punishment on him, enthusiastically. He hadn't noticed the girl watching him when he'd come to watch The Black Lodgers play.

Someone had spilled their beer on the floor and he slipped on it. Legs kicked out in front of him, a near reverse somersault on the hard venue floor.

"Hey, hey, dude . . ."

He was winded.

"You okay?" Female voice. He opened his eyes and saw hers looking down at him. He smiled sheepishly; she smiled back.

"I think I'm dead," he said.

"You will be if you don't get out of the pit," she said.

Isobel helped him up and walked him toward the back of the venue. He wasn't sure what had hurt more, his pride or his back. They found some standing room next to a PA speaker and turned to face each other.

She said, "There are easier ways to get girls to talk to you."

He said, "Huh?" Rubbed at his neck. "Oh."

Isobel turned her head bashfully and smiled toward the ground.

Dresden said, "Hey, thanks. Can I buy you a drink?"

Isobel said, "I . . . um, don't drink alcohol."

"No worries, neither do I," he lied, grinning.

When the show ended, they'd left together in pursuit of soda. They'd found a nearby convenience store, braving through the street's rough denizens, sex workers, beggars and addicts asking for spare change, men peddling weed or harder, and they walked with tall boys of root beer and ginger ale in paper bags. They laughed and named constellations, spoke about their visions of a future that prior to then hadn't included each other, all the stupid wars and politicians, how punk rock held the answer to pretty much anything that ever existed. Hours had felt like minutes. Dawn began to creep on them, coating everything pink.

"So pretty," she said, looking over the city from a spot they'd found in a park.

Dresden said, "Yeah," looking at her. Isobel turned to him and stuck her tongue out. He brushed her hair back and poked her lightly on the nose. "Boop."

Isobel started to laugh and he leaned in and kissed her.

II

"I love you," she whispered, twitching in her sleep. Isobel had tossed and turned all night. She jolted awake. Her heart raced and a cold sweat laced her flesh.

"Pleasant dream or a nightmare?" Pete asked.

"W-what?" Isobel rubbed at her eyes.

"You muttered 'I love you' and tossed around like you were being attacked. I couldn't tell what kind of dream it was." He shrugged. "Ah, no matter." Moonlight came in through the gas station's windows.

"You were watching me sleep." Isobel squinted at him, mockingly.

"I couldn't sleep myself. Thought I'd stare at the moon and let my head wander some." He turned back to the window. "Tomorrow this shelter might be gone, evaporated or burned up or whatever, and we'll have to relocate, assuming we're even here. But that moon . . . that moon's been constant. It's the only thing resembling home we've got left, you ask me."

Isobel's leg only distantly throbbed. They'd wrapped her up with gauze and treated the wound. Given her some painkillers. But she knew that was only a temporary relief. . . .

Isobel said, "What were you thinking about?"

"Oh, everything. And nothing. All at the same time. The mind is strange place." He looked down at his wedding ring.

"You're married."

Pete nodded. "Once."

"Where is she?"

Pete didn't reply.

"Or he . . ."

Pete chuckled. "She. Her name was Martha." He took a deep breath, smiled. "Woman was my heart. Real tough one. Could take you down with just her eyes."

"Is she, is she still alive?"

Pete sniffed. "Nah. She passed long ago."

"Kids?"

He shook his head. "No kids. Always wanted them though. She had the heart attack before we ever got the chance."

"You never remarried?"

Pete laughed, his face brighter now. "Where do you go from the top of the mountain?" He coughed. "Never got what she saw in me, I'll give you that."

"You're a good man, Pete. Any person with a semblance of consciousness could see that. She was lucky to have to have found you." She gave his shoulder a slight squeeze.

"Oh, tosh. Now you're just blowing air up my skirt." They both chuckled.

Pete said, "What about you?"

"His name's Dresden."

"He would have liked you in that dress."

"He already saw me in this dress."

Pete chuckled with his hand over his mouth. "That's bad luck."

"Tell me about it."

Pete listened to her talk about Dresden's disappearance, the Tower of Chapels, his mother. "No," Pete would harshly whisper. He made fierce eye contact with Isobel. He was like a teenage girl who had just heard the latest gossip. Isobel asked about Martha but he insisted she talk about Dresden. Pete said, "You want to hold those memories as close as you can. Martha's still with me up here." He tapped the side of his head. "Lovers who are meant to be with each other can always feel what the other person is feeling. It's like a psychic connection or something," Pete vigorously nodded his head. "If he was dead, I think you'd know. Close your eyes, tell me what you feel."

Isobel cocked her head at Pete.

"I'm serious! Close your eyes, and focus."

She reluctantly sighed and closed her eyes.

"Think of Dresden."

"I will, but you need to shut up so that I can focus," she smiled and turned her head, peaked at Pete with one eye.

Pete muffled his chuckle.

Isobel shut her eyes and imagined him. Saw herself with Dresden, the way things could have happened. Beyond the wedding, a field of grass and flowers, a breeze that blew their hair in their faces. Butterflies rioted in her stomach. Dresden mouthed something to her, something inaudible. Isobel reached out to hold him, but he crumbled away in her arms, carried off by the wind.

III

They ran through tall grass, holding hands. They ran in the sunlight. They laughed. He picked her up and spun her in the middle of the field. He pulled her tight and caressed her face. She said his name, her voice loud in his head. Dresden . . .

"Dresden." He jolted awake.

He was still naked, cold in the water. It was quiet around him and he didn't want to turn on the light. He knew he was alone. The voice had been in his dream, where he wished he was now. But he was still here. Dresden had fallen asleep in the company of his siblings, and he remembered what his mother had taken from them all, had taken from him—

"Isobel," he whispered to the room.

IV

Isobel opened her eyes and said, "My gut tells me he's dead."

"And?"

"My brain refuses to listen."

She looked at Pete and gulped hard.

"I want him to be alive." Isobel started to cry. "I want that."

Pete pulled her in for an embrace and gently patted the back of her head as she cried in his arms.

Six
THE WORLD
IS DEAD

I

Isobel woke up in Pete's arms. Having slept at an awkward angle, her body ached. She wiggled out of the embrace and sat up to stretch. Still groggy, she yawned and stretched out her arms. Behind her, something thudded. Isobel spun around and saw Pete motionless on the floor.

"Pete."

No response. She patted him, thinking him asleep.

"Pete?"

Isobel saw the rash had extended up his neck. With his eyes closed, a slight smile on his face, he looked peaceful. Isobel checked his pulse and confirmed it. Pressed her hand to his heart and told him he was back with his wife. Her eyes watered but nothing came of it. She suppressed the crying fit and turned to see the pooch-bellied cowboy seeing what she was looking at.

"He's passed," said Isobel.

The girl in the pink hoodie said, "What?"

The lady in the sundress who'd taken the role of nurse came over and checked. Nodded heavily.

Mack sauntered over and said, "The fuck is going on. Who's de—" and he saw.

"Here too," said the girl in the pink hoodie. "The twins are both gone."

Isobel looked over; the girl was right, but not just dead—the twins were changed, fused, almost melted, into one thing. Isobel held her hand over her mouth. Closed her eyes.

She'd already seen so much, and maybe they all had, but she wasn't sure how much more she could handle.

Mack said, "Less mouths to feed," and Isobel slapped him. "Bitch, you try that again and," he trailed.

"And you'll what, exactly," Isobel said.

Mack slid his hand to his pistol's holster and grinned.

"People are more than 'a mouth to feed,' and the children . . ."

Mack turned his head down. The others crowded them.

"Pete was a good man," the lady in the sundress said.

"I know it," Mack said. "I just . . ."

"You just what." Isobel got up close, face to face.

"Everything's gone to shit. I've never been good at—"

"Well you better learn to be. We're all that's left."

Mack took off his hat, held it to his chest and sighed.

"Should we bury them?" the cowboy asked.

"What's the point," said Mack. "They'll rot faster than they'll stink."

"I think we should bury them," Isobel said.

Mack eyed her. "You got a shovel?"

"No, I guess not."

Mack said, "What if we wrap them in blankets?"

"We could do that. It's something."

Pete's skin had turned purplish, waxy. Eyes recessed into his skull. His body hardening. The twins were the same way. They'd laid them down beside each other to keep them straight. Mack covered Pete with a wool blanket; the lady in the sundress and the girl in the hoodie covered the twins together, tucked them into it.

The lady in the sundress leaned against a shelf, staring into space, silent.

"Guys," the cowboy said. He held out his arm and rolled up his sleeve. He muttered, "Oh god, not this," and the flesh of his hand rotted to the bone, and the bones went to dust and the disease worked its way up the arm. He screamed and then they all screamed, and then he went quiet and the rest of him dissolved, as if in acid, and burned away. The young man in the jeans and blue shirt crouched in a corner and rocked. He said, "Only a matter of time for the rest of us," and the rest stood wordless, staring at where the cowboy had stood. Then the ground shook and the silence ended.

"Better get a move on," Mack said.

Isobel didn't need to be told twice. The walls of the mini mart wheezed and groaned, came alive as everything else had, and grew sick. She limped behind the others, feeling the twinge of infection in her leg.

Fuck. Is this really it?

The building collapsed and they stood in the middle of the broken road, dust swirling all around them. They'd only gotten some of their weapons. Everything else, food and supplies had gone down with the building. Isobel found herself missing rain. She couldn't remember the last time she'd eaten. Found herself wondering suddenly if there was an afterlife, if Dresden was there, hoping he was. That they'd find each other there. The wind picked up and for the first time, Isobel looked into the distance and noticed that mountains, parts of the scenery she'd long accepted as the backdrop were diminished or gone, that the large peaks had been eaten away by the very same thing that had taken the cowboy and Pete, the twins, and likely everyone she'd ever met. Everything she'd ever known.

The ground rumbled again and the posts holding stoplights in the road shook, began to crumble and a line snapped. The stoplight swung down and hit the lady in the sundress, taking off her head. Isobel gasped. One of the others screamed. Mack grunted and stepped away from the posts. Her body twitched in the street and sprayed from the neck. Blood pooled around the fallen stoplight, the head crushed beneath. Someone said, "Fucking hell," and someone else said, "What the—"

Mack spit and said, "What a waste."

The girl in the hoodie retched. Isobel put an arm on her shoulder and the girl brushed it off angrily. "It's all useless," she muttered, crying now. "W-we can't save ourselves from this."

"She's right, you know," the young man in blue said. "What's the fucking point," and he held up his shotgun under his chin and pulled the trigger. The top of his head fountained up gore. He fell to the ground, knees first and landed sideways.

The girl in the hoodie dove for the shotgun. "See what I mean?" Raised it at the rest of them, deliberated, and then they watched her run off down the street, disappearing into the distance. The survivors started to chatter.

Mack fired his gun into the air. Shouted at the rest of them, "Any of the rest of y'all think about losing your shit—"

The sky crackled, that familiar sound of old speakers. Mack went silent; everyone glanced around to see where the sound had come from. Isobel looked up.

"It's snowing," Mack muttered. "It's fucking snowing. Can you believe it?"

Isobel caught a flake and rubbed it between her fingers. Grey tint spread across her fingers. "Ashes."

A pregnant woman screamed and pointed. Everyone turned and saw the creatures. The ground below them rumbled. Isobel glanced at Mack and he nodded. The ground started to sink in behind them, a massive hole in the pavement. An old rusted car fell in the hole and it began to expand.

"We've been so loud," said Isobel.

There looked to be hundreds of them, as though they'd started to come together in more than just packs.

"There's so many," Mack said, checking his pistol.

"You see that sinkhole?" Isobel asked. "It's getting really big."

"Rock and a hard place, sweetheart." Mack winked.

More sinkholes caved in the distance, swallowed houses, cars. One of the other survivors, a bearded man in a trucker hat, fired into the horde of creatures.

Isobel gripped the metal bar she'd come to find comfort in. Looked into the swarm and hated them and didn't know why.

Mack said, "Good thing assholes don't die first in horror movies," and pulled back the slide of his gun. Isobel wanted to laugh but couldn't. She was going to die here and knew it. The ground shook again, harder this time and everything went still. She heard a rushing sound, like a dam bursting. "What's that?" Mack fired at a creature and missed. Fired again and it fell. The sinkholes erupted with blood, red geysers that touched the sky. Isobel stopped fighting. Everything around her happening in jagged motion, like a flipbook. People who were now monsters fighting people who were in various stages of rot. Nothing seemed real. Isobel looked down at her leg and saw the gangrene had started to set in. Mack shoved her down and shot a creature that had come up on her in the cheek. He pulled the trigger again and saw he was out. Muttered, "Goddamnit," and pulled Isobel to her feet.

"But the others . . ." Isobel said.

"Look around you." They were overrun. "You okay to run or do I need to carry you?" He smirked, put the empty pistol back in its holster.

"In your dreams, jerk." The new splint on Isobel's leg was holding up. The lady in the sundress had duct-taped two halves of a broom handle tightly. The look on her face when she'd removed the femur and blood-soaked strips of her dress . . . Isobel held the emotion and put her arm over Mack's shoulder. Screams filled the air.

"You've been bit," she said, seeing his arm.

"So?" Mack hocked and spit. "They're just rich folk, not zombies."

Isobel limped as fast as she could and noticed the pain had stopped coming. It wasn't that the healing had happened, she supposed, rather that the nerves had deteriorated around the break. Still, she wished she could run. Didn't understand why Mack was keeping pace with her while he was still able. They hadn't gotten very far when part of the mob had started to trickle out, following them.

Mack looked behind them and saw the futility. "Keep your eyes up ahead."

"Wait," Isobel slowed down. "What is *that* . . . ?"

Mack, aggravated, turned back the way they were headed, where the road had dissolved into the dusty ground that had been so many things just days before. "Don't know."

Geysers still burst red from sinkholes in the distance. The sun looked weak on the horizon, like it too was dying out. Isobel held tight to the length of rebar that'd started to feel to her like security. They approached the object in the dust, undiminished, a solitary form in what had become a bleeding desert. It looked like an old fashioned elevator. Barred metal, clean, with manual doors and a latch. Its door was open like it'd been waiting. The interior was modestly finished, trimmed with stained wood and velvet floors.

"Must have been part of a building," Mack said, breathing erratic from the pace.

Isobel wasn't convinced and she knew he wasn't either.

"Could give us some cover," he added.

Behind them the creatures gained. More sinkholes erupted as others ceased to spurt the planet's blood and collapsed inward, emptied. Isobel finally looked behind her, mouth agape. They reached the elevator door and Mack grabbed the metal rod out of her hand, shoved her hard into the elevator and pulled the doors shut. Doors latched loudly.

He said, "Maybe it's better down there than up here."

Isobel looked to the ground, uncertain. She said, "What if it's worse?"

He said, "Then I'm sorry." He coughed. The elevator began to descend.

"I underestimated you," she said, knowing it was no use to argue.

"Don't tell anyone." He turned back to face the outside, striking a confident stance as she watched. Then elevator dipped beyond the view of outside and she could see only the rough concrete walls of the shaft. The cables stuttered but it seemed to have survived the deterioration of everything else. It went on a while and she sat, waiting, listening to an electrical hum. When the door finally opened, it opened to a darkly lit tunnel. Isobel righted herself and walked out into it. The elevator stayed put and whatever force that had brought it down shut off and it got quiet. The tunnel led her toward light, and like a moth she couldn't resist its pull.

II

Dresden had gone in and out of sleep, trapped in the trophy room.

The room's exit had disappeared sometime in the night. Like every other confused junction in this labyrinth, he'd known it would be one way. The lights had ceased to function anymore and he didn't know if they'd burnt out or if he'd only imagined clapping. The bodies of his brothers and sisters had not yet begun to stink and he wondered if he'd starve to death before the stench arrived. It wasn't a pleasant thought.

He closed his eyes and felt himself drift.

Above him, in the ventilation duct, a form crawled like a slug. It knew what he had done. Could smell the guilt on him. It pried open the grate just enough to squeeze through and its body hung from the edge by little hooked tendrils that'd once been fingers. It secreted a line and lowered itself down slowly into the room. It met Dresden's sleeping frame and found his back. Smelled the blood, a familiar taste. The tendrils injected him with an anesthetic and attached themselves, pulled the parasite in closer and gave it a home.

He had bad dreams.

66

III

Isobel emerged into what looked like a hoarder's paradise: mountains of junk towered over herself, more akin to a scrap yard than a storage facility. It looked to her like a collection of artifacts, of history—famous paintings, choice sports cars, ancient statues, an impeccably preserved eastern galley, so much more. All pinnacle, like they'd been stripped from time and hadn't aged.

"It's the beginnings of a catalogue," said a low voice from somewhere, maybe everywhere around her.

Isobel walked around the mess, saw a silhouette moving around, found that the path through the collection led to a machine room.

"Hello," she called out.

Something clattered to the ground and steps walked determinedly toward her. Isobel hobbled away, backed in the opposite direction of the sound. Bumped into the tenant of this place and jumped, nearly screamed. It was him, the man from the television . . . the feeling, the thing in the corner of her eye. He wore massive bottle cap glasses. He came at her and she stumbled backward, trying to dodge the machinery blindly and caught her hair in the tracks. Metal teeth pulled her closer, held her. She tried to push away and couldn't.

He whispered, "You . . ."

Isobel began to panic, confused and trapped. He vanished immediately, blipped into a diminishing ball of light, then nothing, like a tube television that'd just been turned off. He reappeared on the other side of her, a foot away, startling her again. Was he a ghost, or worse? He was much shorter than her. His face was round under thick glasses, mouth agape, scentless hot breath escaping his lips and blanketing her face.

The tension pulled chunks of her from her scalp. Immense pain shot through her head and she put her hands to her hair and pulled away harder. Too much hair had been caught. Isobel clenched her teeth and groaned and felt her head close to the gears now.

The man leaned in and awkwardly inspected her from head to toe.

"You're in need of repair," he said.

Isobel didn't say anything back.

He blipped and she watched him reappear and disappear again at different points of the room. He seemed to be observing her.

Isobel twisted around as far as she could manage and pushed her arms out in front of her, pushing away. Pressed her feet against the machine's platform. Isobel screamed as her hair tore out, taking chunks of skin with it. She felt the blood trickle down her back from her head. Turned back to the man and he was gone.

Everything seemed green-hued down here, hazy, she realized.

Isobel shook the throbbing pain out of her mind. "What, what is this place?"

He blipped behind her, holding a leather-bound book of nursery rhymes.

"This is interesting literature," he said. "Nonsensical but enjoyable."

"Who are you?"

"There are codes in the rhymes. It will take too long to explain them to you."

"How did you keep this place from being consumed?"

"I've watched everything."

"I don't understand."

"This. This is my occupation."

Isobel pulled up her hood to cover the torn scalp. "The televisions and radios . . . how did you do that?" She stepped toward him and he blipped behind her, no longer holding the book.

"This," the man spread his arms out, gesturing at the entire underground structure, "is my ark."

"Like in the myth with the animals?"

"I preserve information."

"Who are you?"

"I am god," he said, his expression deadpan.

They stared at each other for a moment.

Isobel said, "Are you serious?"

He shook his head. "No, that was a joke."

"Why am I here?"

"Finally." He motioned for her to follow. "I want to show you something."

Where he took her was the center of the ark, where it branched into several other tunnels. Isobel assumed that they led to other catalogued areas and wondered just how many things, from how many times, were in this place. He blipped from beside her to a control panel. There were thousands of dots on a board, only a few of them still lit.

He said, "These were access points. The way you came, that was this one." He pointed to a point that was now dim.

"The elevator?"

"Sometimes an elevator, sometimes a door. Other things."

"Why are only some of the lights on?"

"When somewhere ceases to exist, there's no longer a door to it."

"You invited me down here, didn't you."

"I can reunite you," he said.

Isobel's heart sank. "What do you mean?"

"Billions of people in this world and I warned them all that this was coming."

"How many are there now?"

"You are the only one who heard me."

"I . . ."

"To be a caretaker of so many lives, to be so ignored ."

"And you mean to say that you can bring me to him. That he is still alive."

"Yes."

He blipped ahead. Her movement kept uneven rhythm over the metal floor as she trudged forward. He motioned to one of the other tunnels and she followed. The tunnel took them past a taxidermied Tyrannosaurus rex and a giant penny, an endless stack of books. At the end of the tunnel wasn't an elevator, but an old wooden coffin. He pointed to it and blipped away.

Not knowing what else to do, Isobel reluctantly stepped into the coffin, lowered herself to a seated position and then lay back. She took a deep breath and held it. Pulled the flimsy dry rotted lid down over her and waited.

Nothing happened.

Isobel tried to push open the coffin lid and couldn't. It was stuck. She hit it and her fist went through. Dirt spilled in. Felt beads of sweat on her brow. Isobel's heart raced and she closed her eyes to relax. Dresden. She imagined him in her mind, the way she'd last seen him. She missed him so much. The history of their lives spun around in her mind like a carousel. She whispered his name again and again. The lid's rotten wood gave and she started to dig.

IV

He slept against the wall with his legs tucked to his chest. He rocked back and forth in the room's darkness and waited. He heard the house's rumbling and jolted awake.

How long have I been out?

It felt like he'd dreamt an eternity. He didn't think he'd ever understand time again. His mother's voice felt distant, echoing in his head as if that were the nightmare he'd woken from and this room's darkness were the only reprieve, alone among the corpses of his only family. *A son should love his mother . . .*

"You win, *mother*," he whispered.

The walls around him shook again and he wondered if it was an earthquake.

An entrance materialized across the room, where the hall had once been, only it led to stairs and brightness . . .

He stood and felt weak and fell back to his knees. Thought of Isobel and found the will to rise again. Could not look at his siblings as he walked past them toward the light. Is this death, he wondered. Finally come.

III

Her right hand emerged first, the skin peeling from it, bone showing, and then came the rest of her, birthed from the soil and into the unfamiliar courtyard. It took a moment for her eyes to adjust. The disease had found her and was working its way through. She'd seen how this went.

On one end of the courtyard, it seemed as if there was only space. The ground simply ended and led only toward stars and blueness. The sun felt weak on her skin. Isobel stood unevenly, the brace breaking down around her leg. The small man had said Dresden would be there, but she was alone. The other end of the courtyard was a house, a mansion that had only just started being consumed, its edges slowly charring. Ashes rained from the sky around her.

A butterfly fluttered past in a diagonal pattern and she stopped to watch it. Had thought insects extinct, everything extinct but her. Isobel held out her hand and the butterfly settled on it for a moment before moving on.

IV

He emerged into the courtyard. Long lines of tall trees like a forest's hall. He felt the fresh air and laughed. Apart from what looked like dirty snow falling from the sky, this seemed like a cruel joke, another bad dream, this pleasantness. He thought he heard something. His name. Dresden stared far out into lines of trees, tried to discern between shapes that danced like shadows.

He imagined her coming toward him, could see her so clearly.

"Isobel," he said.

But the figure of his dream stopped in her tracks, seemed to be falling apart. He moved toward her and she began to back away, horrified at his being there.

V

Isobel hesitated. Where had the small man sent her? This vision of Dresden perverted, naked and monstrous, heads rising up out of his back, tendrils flittering behind him.

VI

Dresden called out, "Isobel!"

He felt the weight on his back, felt winded. He slowed down and panted. Reached behind him and patted at his back and became afraid. The symbiote was growing out of his back like a tumor. He felt anger where he imagined there should have been fear. Balled his hands into tight fists and his nails dug deep into his palms. He hit at the thing on his back and it screeched, but he felt its hooks pull deeper into the meat of his back. He yelled out in pain. Steeled himself and took hold of the creature and pulled on it, pain surging through his body. He pulled harder and he felt it tear flesh as it came loose.

He threw it over his head and it landed on the ground in front of him with a thud. He realized how small it was, the size of a small child, its body covered in tar and boils. Skin bleached gray, riddled with black veins. It quivered and heads began to emerge out of, what he realized, had been a human's upper torso. Limbs charred away. It took a moment to recognize, because the heads had seemed almost digested, as though this were only the beginning of a metamorphosis.

"Elise?" Memories of every injection he'd ever witnessed suddenly crossed his mind. Her leaking gloves. Whatever was supposed to be keeping her alive had turned on her or was intentional . . .

The symbiote cocked its center head, bumping one of the side heads and cooed. The others, Dresden realized, were the doctor and nurse. They'd somehow fused. Only they looked vacant, more absorbed into whatever this body was changing into, their faces frozen in contorted expressions. His mother dominant. Elise shook her head and looked at Dresden, eyes pleading. The symbiote's tendrils pointed to the base of its torso, where the womb would be. Making motions that almost seemed to welcome him back into it.

Dresden said, "You really never got it." He'd have run, were it anything beyond her; he had ceased to be afraid of his mother. "Do you honestly think you're still my mother?"

The symbiote hissed, tendrils flailing wild.

"I just feel sad for y—"

The ground shook. He looked past the symbiote to the figure that was headed unevenly toward them. The ground seemed to quiver, moved in waves that threw them all off-balance. The figure was dressed in black and white, hobbling weakly. Was he really imagining this? Before him, the woman who'd taken everything away . . . and yet there, the thing he wanted, no, needed most, coming through the trees and ashes now.

His heart raced. As if sensing this, the symbiote turned, his mother's dying face, burning angry, recessing back into the body, absorbing the other heads, emerging in a burst of fluid through the torsos center as a wide mouth with hundreds of tiny teeth.

Whatever fear he thought he'd vanquished returned instantly.

Almost felt his mother saying, *if I can't have you . . .*

He waved his arm toward Isobel and tried to warn her, shouting. The ground rocked them again and his mother began to transform further, the veins beneath her skin growing thicker, pulsing with whatever passed for blood in that mutant form. Hands wetly emerged on all sides of her, cancerously grew into arms, dripped with bile, expelling the charred stubs where the old limbs had been. Dresden watched terrified, frozen. His mother reoriented and darted across the path. Dresden shouted, "No!" Ran after Elise, unsure of just what he could do, while the ground imploded behind Isobel.

VII

The ground crumbled away behind her at a rapid pace. Isobel turned back, saw the emerging abyss, turned forward toward where the nightmare was, stuck. Except it was no longer Dresden that frightened her, it was the thing that had come off of him, scared him back like a rabid dog, and now came down the hill rushing her.

Dresden followed, shouting behind it.

Isobel coughed, lungs burning. Her heart pumped acetone and fire.

She'd come so far and there he was and *oh god what the fuck is that?*

It looked like a snapping mouth with thousands of tails flailing, running on arms like a spider after its prey. Isobel felt around for the metal rod, the rebar she'd had, and she remembered that Mack had taken it. The symbiote hurled itself through the air at her, took her down, snapping at her face. Isobel threw up her arms and blocked the bite, cutting up her arms. Its tendrils touched her skin and hardened, pulsed, bit in and pulled the symbiote closer. Isobel felt blood draining from her. Looked down and watched shark like teeth biting at her arms. Isobel went faint, saw static, crashed.

VIII

Elise had taken her down, attached to her, was *eating* her. Dresden did the only thing he could do: he got angry.

He found a branch off to the side of the path, between some trees. Held it like a club and swung it at his mother. Connected once and got no reaction. He shouted and swung again. The branch connected with the torso's spine and the tendrils flittered wild. His mother shrieked. The tendrils hardened, spiked out and struck Dresden. He fell back, coughing. Dozens of punctures across his upper body seeped. The symbiote sensed this and withdrew from Isobel, turned to face her son, watched him stumble back with fatal injuries. Elise wailed, the mouth in the torso's chest wide open. Backed away from her son, past Isobel, in disbelief at what she'd done. Dresden was her last child. Her only child. She let out another wail and the ground beneath her caved and she fell, tumbling down into the dark, alone.

Isobel opened her eyes slowly. Her hands and forearms had been eaten at. Body bleeding from what seemed like everywhere. *What made it stop?* She felt the tremors growing, but didn't know if the shaking was her or the ground.

Isobel got to her feet and saw him.

"Oh no," she whimpered. "Oh no . . ."

Seven
INTO NOTHING

I

Dresden rolled on to his side so that he may better be able to look at Isobel.

"How should we die?" he asked.

Isobel, still on her back with her eyes closed, furrowed her face, stuck out her tongue and played dead. Dresden chuckled. Reached over and pushed in her tongue with a finger. Isobel made a sour face and chuckled. "I'm cured! Wait, were you being serious?"

"Sure," he shrugged.

Isobel traced designs over the grass.

"I want love to be what kills me."

Dresden said, "What a sap."

Isobel playfully shoved him, grabbed a handful of grass and yanked it out and threw it on him. "Seriously. Love affects you physically. Makes your heart race, stomach tickle, legs weak . . ." She exhaled slowly. "Why couldn't it kill you?"

"So what you're saying is you're not that in love with me." Dresden snickered.

"How do you figure?"

"You're still alive."

"Shut up." Isobel rolled her eyes. "So maybe I'm a sap. It'd also be romantic to die in the arms of a lover. You know, have that togetherness be the last thing you feel."

Dresden climbed over Isobel, straddled her. Kissed her.

She muttered into his lips, "I will fucking kill you."

"Meh," he pulled away. "There are way worse ways to go."

Dresden brushed the hair from Isobel's face and pulled her in for another kiss. He guessed this was happiness.

II

Isobel took Dresden's hand. He looked up at her weakly and smiled. Blood soaked into the gravel and dirt beneath him. The edge was coming up on them now and she knew that this was the furthest they'd get from it. Neither of them had the capacity to carry the other. Isobel thought, *We're so boned.* Dresden saw her with the hood down, the bleeding scalp, rotten at the back of her head. He whispered almost inaudibly, "Nice hair, babe."

Isobel looked him over, ran her hand over his chest and said, "Hey, nice outfit."

Dresden said, "I wore it for you," and breathed shallow. "Heh." He saw the wedding dress and she thought he was going to cry. "But yours is . . ." Dresden coughed up blood, his voice syrup thick. ". . . better."

Isobel squeezed his hand. "I wish we had more time."

That sinking wasn't far. Beyond it, Isobel saw the stars, some of them familiar constellations. Their light was so far away that it was true some of them had already been dead before it ever reached them. She wondered if their sun looked like that to the other side of the galaxy.

He said, "I'm so tired."

Isobel said, "Me too, me too."

She kept the rotten hand behind her back. Hoped he wouldn't see it, but he saw her avoiding and asked to see it, knowing her better than she'd thought. His face went slack when he saw the gangrene; it had spread farther up her arm. He said, "Oh no, you caught it," and pulled the hand forward and kissed it. "I'll make it better." The hoodie's sleeves were in tatters. She took it off and covered him with it. Isobel started to cry. Dresden said, "What's wrong?"

"N-nothing."

Ahead of them, the house imploded under its own weight. Had let out a sound like a scream before it folded in on itself and evaporated, its dust floating out to space. *How is it possible we're still breathing?* It seemed impossible. Likely, the small man would have known, but he was gone now. There were no more doors.

Dresden tried to sit up and couldn't. "I can't move. Why can't I move?"

The ground seemed to almost cough and shudder the way it shook. The ashes had ceased to fall for some time now.

"Shhh," she said and kissed the top of his head.

Dresden looked up at Isobel with a smile on his face. He looked weak. He closed his eyes and went limp in her arms. Isobel whimpered, bawling now. She sniffled and cradled his head to her chest and stroked his hair. A hardness, like a knot, tightened in her chest. Isobel sat up and waited. Dresden was gone and she was alone. It all seemed so meaningless. The ground beneath her began to give. Isobel thought she'd be back with him soon enough.

"I love you," she whispered to the corpse.

Eigh . . .
THE E . . .

Tiffany Scandal is a writer, photographer, and model who lives in Portland, Oregon with her three black cats. In her spare time, she conjures up dark forces, drinks whiskey and hangs out with naked ladies. She enjoys things that make her feel uneasy. One day she imagines her house will be filled with books and cats, and she'll get to tell you stories that put sailors to shame.

Her short fiction has appeared in The Magazine of Bizarro Fiction and a chapbook titled Hostile Awakenings. Her photography and modeling have appeared both online and in print. This is her first novella.

Visit her online at www.TiffanyScandalSucks.

BIZARRO BOOKS

CATALOG   SPRING 2013

ERASERHEAD PRESS

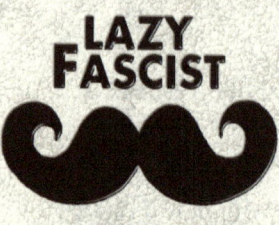

Your major resource for the bizarro fiction genre:

WWW.BIZARROCENTRAL.COM

Introduce yourselves to the bizarro fiction genre and all of its authors with the Bizarro Starter Kit series. Each volume features short novels and short stories by ten of the leading bizarro authors, designed to give you a perfect sampling of the genre for only $10.

BB-0X1
"The Bizarro Starter Kit" (Orange)

Featuring D. Harlan Wilson, Carlton Mellick III, Jeremy Robert Johnson, Kevin L Donihe, Gina Ranalli, Andre Duza, Vincent W. Sakowski, Steve Beard, John Edward Lawson, and Bruce Taylor. **236 pages $10**

BB-0X2
"The Bizarro Starter Kit" (Blue)

Featuring Ray Fracalossy, Jeremy C. Shipp, Jordan Krall, Mykle Hansen, Andersen Prunty, Eckhard Gerdes, Bradley Sands, Steve Aylett, Christian TeBordo, and Tony Rauch. **244 pages $10**

BB-0X2
"The Bizarro Starter Kit" (Purple)

Featuring Russell Edson, Athena Villaverde, David Agranoff, Matthew Revert, Andrew Goldfarb, Jeff Burk, Garrett Cook, Kris Saknussemm, Cody Goodfellow, and Cameron Pierce **264 pages $10**

BB-001 **"The Kafka Effekt" D. Harlan Wilson** — A collection of forty-four irreal short stories loosely written in the vein of Franz Kafka, with more than a pinch of William S. Burroughs sprinkled on top. **211 pages $14**

BB-002 **"Satan Burger" Carlton Mellick III** — The cult novel that put Carlton Mellick III on the map ... Six punks get jobs at a fast food restaurant owned by the devil in a city violently overpopulated by surreal alien cultures. **236 pages $14**

BB-003 **"Some Things Are Better Left Unplugged" Vincent Sakwoski** — Join The Man and his Nemesis, the obese tabby, for a nightmare roller coaster ride into this postmodern fantasy. **152 pages $10**

BB-005 **"Razor Wire Pubic Hair" Carlton Mellick III** — A genderless humandildo is purchased by a razor dominatrix and brought into her nightmarish world of bizarre sex and mutilation. **176 pages $11**

BB-007 **"The Baby Jesus Butt Plug" Carlton Mellick III** — Using clones of the Baby Jesus for anal sex will be the hip sex fetish of the future. **92 pages $10**

BB-010 **"The Menstruating Mall" Carlton Mellick III** — "The Breakfast Club meets Chopping Mall as directed by David Lynch." - Brian Keene **212 pages $12**

BB-011 **"Angel Dust Apocalypse" Jeremy Robert Johnson** — Meth-heads, man-made monsters, and murderous Neo-Nazis. "Seriously amazing short stories..." - Chuck Palahniuk, author of Fight Club **184 pages $11**

BB-015 **"Foop!" Chris Genoa** — Strange happenings are going on at Dactyl, Inc, the world's first and only time travel tourism company.
"A surreal pie in the face!" - Christopher Moore **300 pages $14**

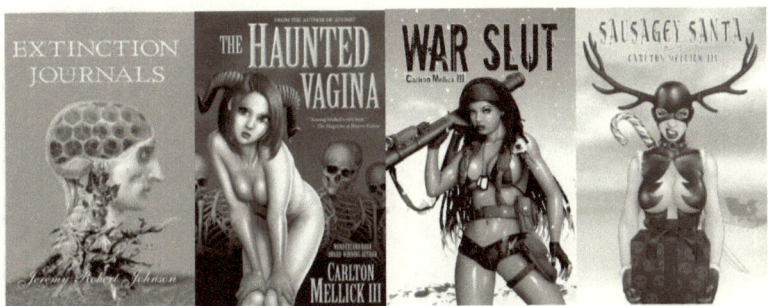

BB-032 **"Extinction Journals" Jeremy Robert Johnson** — An uncanny voyage across a newly nuclear America where one man must confront the problems associated with loneliness, insane dieties, radiation, love, and an ever-evolving cockroach suit with a mind of its own. **104 pages $10**

BB-037 **"The Haunted Vagina" Carlton Mellick III** — It's difficult to love a woman whose vagina is a gateway to the world of the dead. **132 pages $10**

BB-043 **"War Slut" Carlton Mellick III** — Part "1984," part "Waiting for Godot," and part action horror video game adaptation of John Carpenter's "The Thing." **116 pages $10**

BB-047 **"Sausagey Santa" Carlton Mellick III** — A bizarro Christmas tale featuring Santa as a piratey mutant with a body made of sausages. 124 pages $10

BB-048 **"Misadventures in a Thumbnail Universe" Vincent Sakowski** — Dive deep into the surreal and satirical realms of neo-classical Blender Fiction, filled with television shoes and flesh-filled skies. **120 pages $10**

BB-053 **"Ballad of a Slow Poisoner" Andrew Goldfarb** — Millford Mutterwurst sat down on a Tuesday to take his afternoon tea, and made the unpleasant discovery that his elbows were becoming flatter. **128 pages $10**

BB-055 **"Help! A Bear is Eating Me" Mykle Hansen** — The bizarro, heartwarming, magical tale of poor planning, hubris and severe blood loss... **150 pages $11**

BB-056 **"Piecemeal June" Jordan Krall** — A man falls in love with a living sex doll, but with love comes danger when her creator comes after her with crab-squid assassins. **90 pages $9**

BB-058 **"The Overwhelming Urge" Andersen Prunty** — A collection of bizarro tales by Andersen Prunty. **150 pages $11**

BB-059 **"Adolf in Wonderland" Carlton Mellick III** — A dreamlike adventure that takes a young descendant of Adolf Hitler's design and sends him down the rabbit hole into a world of imperfection and disorder. **180 pages $11**

BB-061 **"Ultra Fuckers" Carlton Mellick III** — Absurdist suburban horror about a couple who enter an upper middle class gated community but can't find their way out. **108 pages $9**

BB-062 **"House of Houses" Kevin L. Donihe** — An odd man wants to marry his house. Unfortunately, all of the houses in the world collapse at the same time in the Great House Holocaust. Now he must travel to House Heaven to find his departed fiancee. **172 pages $11**

BB-064 **"Squid Pulp Blues" Jordan Krall** — In these three bizarro-noir novellas, the reader is thrown into a world of murderers, drugs made from squid parts, deformed gun-toting veterans, and a mischievous apocalyptic donkey. **204 pages $12**

BB-065 **"Jack and Mr. Grin" Andersen Prunty** — "When Mr. Grin calls you can hear a smile in his voice. Not a warm and friendly smile, but the kind that seizes your spine in fear. You don't need to pay your phone bill to hear it. That smile is in every line of Prunty's prose." - Tom Bradley. **208 pages $12**

BB-066 **"Cybernetrix" Carlton Mellick III** — What would you do if your normal everyday world was slowly mutating into the video game world from Tron? **212 pages $12**

BB-072 **"Zerostrata" Andersen Prunty** — Hansel Nothing lives in a tree house, suffers from memory loss, has a very eccentric family, and falls in love with a woman who runs naked through the woods every night. **144 pages $11**

BB-073 **"The Egg Man" Carlton Mellick III** — It is a world where humans reproduce like insects. Children are the property of corporations, and having an enormous ten-foot brain implanted into your skull is a grotesque sexual fetish. Mellick's industrial urban dystopia is one of his darkest and grittiest to date. **184 pages $11**

BB-074 **"Shark Hunting in Paradise Garden" Cameron Pierce** — A group of strange humanoid religious fanatics travel back in time to the Garden of Eden to discover it is invested with hundreds of giant flying maneating sharks. **150 pages $10**

BB-075 **"Apeshit" Carlton Mellick III -** Friday the 13th meets Visitor Q. Six hipster teens go to a cabin in the woods inhabited by a deformed killer. An incredibly fucked-up parody of B-horror movies with a bizarro slant. **192 pages $12**

BB-076 **"Fuckers of Everything on the Crazy Shitting Planet of the Vomit At mosphere" Mykle Hansen -** Three bizarro satires. Monster Cocks, Journey to the Center of Agnes Cuddlebottom, and Crazy Shitting Planet. **228 pages $12**

BB-077 **"The Kissing Bug" Daniel Scott Buck** — In the tradition of Roald Dahl, Tim Burton, and Edward Gorey, comes this bizarro anti-war children's story about a bohemian conenose kissing bug who falls in love with a human woman. **116 pages $10**

BB-078 **"MachoPoni" Lotus Rose** — It's My Little Pony... *Bizarro* style! A long time ago Poniworld was split in two. On one side of the Jagged Line is the Pastel Kingdom, a magical land of music, parties, and positivity. On the other side of the Jagged Line is Dark Kingdom inhabited by an army of undead ponies. **148 pages $11**

BB-079 **"The Faggiest Vampire" Carlton Mellick III** — A Roald Dahl-esque children's story about two faggy vampires who partake in a mustache competition to find out which one is truly the faggiest. **104 pages $10**

BB-080 **"Sky Tongues" Gina Ranalli** — The autobiography of Sky Tongues, the biracial hermaphrodite actress with tongues for fingers. Follow her strange life story as she rises from freak to fame. **204 pages $12**

BB-081 **"Washer Mouth" Kevin L. Donihe** - A washing machine becomes human and pursues his dream of meeting his favorite soap opera star. **244 pages $11**

BB-082 **"Shatnerquake" Jeff Burk** - All of the characters ever played by William Shatner are suddenly sucked into our world. Their mission: hunt down and destroy the real William Shatner. **100 pages $10**

BB-083 **"The Cannibals of Candyland" Carlton Mellick III** - There exists a race of cannibals that are made of candy. They live in an underground world made out of candy. One man has dedicated his life to killing them all. **170 pages $11**

BB-084 **"Slub Glub in the Weird World of the Weeping Willows" Andrew Goldfarb** - The charming tale of a blue glob named Slub Glub who helps the weeping willows whose tears are flooding the earth. There are also hyenas, ghosts, and a voodoo priest **100 pages $10**

BB-085 **"Super Fetus" Adam Pepper** - Try to abort this fetus and he'll kick your ass! **104 pages $10**

BB-086 **"Fistful of Feet" Jordan Krall** - A bizarro tribute to spaghetti westerns, featuring Cthulhu-worshipping Indians, a woman with four feet, a crazed gunman who is obsessed with sucking on candy, Syphilis-ridden mutants, sexually transmitted tattoos, and a house devoted to the freakiest fetishes. **228 pages $12**

BB-087 **"Ass Goblins of Auschwitz" Cameron Pierce** - It's Monty Python meets Nazi exploitation in a surreal nightmare as can only be imagined by Bizarro author Cameron Pierce. **104 pages $10**

BB-088 **"Silent Weapons for Quiet Wars" Cody Goodfellow** - "This is high-end psychological surrealist horror meets bottom-feeding low-life crime in a techno-thrilling science fiction world full of Lovecraft and magic..." -John Skipp **212 pages $12**

BB-089 "Warrior Wolf Women of the Wasteland" Carlton Mellick III — Road Warrior Werewolves versus McDonaldland Mutants...post-apocalyptic fiction has never been quite like this. **316 pages $13**

BB-091 "Super Giant Monster Time" Jeff Burk — A tribute to choose your own adventures and Godzilla movies. Will you escape the giant monsters that are rampaging the fuck out of your city and shit? Or will you join the mob of alien-controlled punk rockers causing chaos in the streets? What happens next depends on you. **188 pages $12**

BB-092 "Perfect Union" Cody Goodfellow — "Cronenberg's THE FLY on a grand scale: human/insect gene-spliced body horror, where the human hive politics are as shocking as the gore." -John Skipp. **272 pages $13**

BB-093 "Sunset with a Beard" Carlton Mellick III — 14 stories of surreal science fiction. **200 pages $12**

BB-094 "My Fake War" Andersen Prunty — The absurd tale of an unlikely soldier forced to fight a war that, quite possibly, does not exist. It's Rambo meets Waiting for Godot in this subversive satire of American values and the scope of the human imagination. **128 pages $11**

BB-095"Lost in Cat Brain Land" Cameron Pierce — Sad stories from a surreal world. A fascist mustache, the ghost of Franz Kafka, a desert inside a dead cat. Primordial entities mourn the death of their child. The desperate serve tea to mysterious creatures. A hopeless romantic falls in love with a pterodactyl. And much more. **152 pages $11**

BB-096 "The Kobold Wizard's Dildo of Enlightenment +2" Carlton Mellick III — A Dungeons and Dragons parody about a group of people who learn they are only made up characters in an AD&D campaign and must find a way to resist their nerdy teenaged players and retarded dungeon master in order to survive. 232 **pages $12**

BB-098 "A Hundred Horrible Sorrows of Ogner Stump" Andrew Goldfarb — Goldfarb's acclaimed comic series. A magical and weird journey into the horrors of everyday life. **164 pages $11**

BB-099 **"Pickled Apocalypse of Pancake Island" Cameron Pierce**—A demented fairy tale about a pickle, a pancake, and the apocalypse. **102 pages $8**

BB-100 **"Slag Attack" Andersen Prunty**— Slag Attack features four visceral, noir stories about the living, crawling apocalypse. A slag is what survivors are calling the slug-like maggots raining from the sky, burrowing inside people, and hollowing out their flesh and their sanity. **148 pages $11**

BB-101 **"Slaughterhouse High" Robert Devereaux**—A place where schools are built with secret passageways, rebellious teens get zippers installed in their mouths and genitals, and once a year, on that special night, one couple is slaughtered and the bits of their bodies are kept as souvenirs. **304 pages $13**

BB-102 **"The Emerald Burrito of Oz" John Skipp & Marc Levinthal** —OZ IS REAL! Magic is real! The gate is really in Kansas! And America is finally allowing Earth tourists to visit this weird-ass, mysterious land. But when Gene of Los Angeles heads off for summer vacation in the Emerald City, little does he know that a war is brewing...a war that could destroy both worlds. **280 pages $13**

BB-103 **"The Vegan Revolution... with Zombies" David Agranoff** — When there's no more meat in hell, the vegans will walk the earth. **160 pages $11**

BB-104 **"The Flappy Parts" Kevin L Donihe**—Poems about bunnies, LSD, and police abuse. You know, things that matter. 132 **pages $11**

BB-105 **"Sorry I Ruined Your Orgy" Bradley Sands**—Bizarro humorist Bradley Sands returns with one of the strangest, most hilarious collections of the year. **130 pages $11**

BB-106 **"Mr. Magic Realism" Bruce Taylor**—Like Golden Age science fiction comics written by Freud, *Mr. Magic Realism* is a strange, insightful adventure that spans the furthest reaches of the galaxy, exploring the hidden caverns in the hearts and minds of men, women, aliens, and biomechanical cats. **152 pages $11**

BB-107 "Zombies and Shit" Carlton Mellick III—"Battle Royale" meets "Return of the Living Dead." Mellick's bizarro tribute to the zombie genre. **308 pages $13**

BB-108 "The Cannibal's Guide to Ethical Living" Mykle Hansen— Over a five star French meal of fine wine, organic vegetables and human flesh, a lunatic delivers a witty, chilling, disturbingly sane argument in favor of eating the rich.. **184 pages $11**

BB-109 "Starfish Girl" Athena Villaverde—In a post-apocalyptic underwater dome society, a girl with a starfish growing from her head and an assassin with sea anenome hair are on the run from a gang of mutant fish men. **160 pages $11**

BB-110 "Lick Your Neighbor" Chris Genoa—Mutant ninjas, a talking whale, kung fu masters, maniacal pilgrims, and an alcoholic clown populate Chris Genoa's surreal, darkly comical and unnerving reimagining of the first Thanksgiving. **303 pages $13**

BB-111 "Night of the Assholes" Kevin L. Donihe—A plague of assholes is infecting the countryside. Normal everyday people are transforming into jerks, snobs, dicks, and douchebags. And they all have only one purpose: to make your life a living hell.. **192 pages $11**

BB-112 "Jimmy Plush, Teddy Bear Detective" Garrett Cook—Hardboiled cases of a private detective trapped within a teddy bear body. **180 pages $11**

BB-113 "The Deadheart Shelters" Forrest Armstrong—The hip hop lovechild of William Burroughs and Dali... **144 pages $11**

BB-114 "Eyeballs Growing All Over Me... Again" Tony Raugh— Absurd, surreal, playful, dream-like, whimsical, and a lot of fun to read. **144 pages $11**

BB-115 **"Whargoul" Dave Brockie** — From the killing grounds of Stalingrad to the death camps of the holocaust. From torture chambers in Iraq to race riots in the United States, the Whargoul was there, killing and raping. **244 pages $12**

BB-116 **"By the Time We Leave Here, We'll Be Friends" J. David Osborne** — A David Lynchian nightmare set in a Russian gulag, where its prisoners, guards, traitors, soldiers, lovers, and demons fight for survival and their own rapidly deteriorating humanity. **168 pages $11**

BB-117 **"Christmas on Crack" edited by Carlton Mellick III** — Perverted Christmas Tales for the whole family! . . . as long as every member of your family is over the age of 18. **168 pages $11**

BB-118 **"Crab Town" Carlton Mellick III** — Radiation fetishists, balloon people, mutant crabs, sail-bike road warriors, and a love affair between a woman and an H-Bomb. This is one mean asshole of a city. Welcome to Crab Town. **100 pages $8**

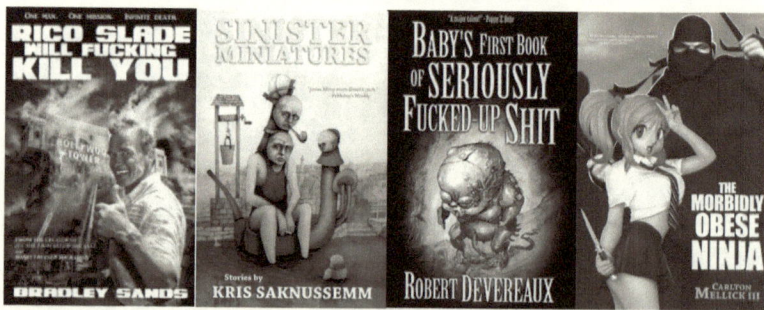

BB-119 **"Rico Slade Will Fucking Kill You" Bradley Sands** — Rico Slade is an action hero. Rico Slade can rip out a throat with his bare hands. Rico Slade's favorite food is the honey-roasted peanut. Rico Slade will fucking kill everyone. A novel. **122 pages $8**

BB-120 **"Sinister Miniatures" Kris Saknussemm** — The definitive collection of short fiction by Kris Saknussemm, confirming that he is one of the best, most daring writers of the weird to emerge in the twenty-first century. **180 pages $11**

BB-121 **"Baby's First Book of Seriously Fucked up Shit" Robert Devereaux** — Ten stories of the strange, the gross, and the just plain fucked up from one of the most original voices in horror. **176 pages $11**

BB-122 **"The Morbidly Obese Ninja" Carlton Mellick III** — These days, if you want to run a successful company . . . you're going to need a lot of ninjas. **92 pages $8**

BB-123 "Abortion Arcade" Cameron Pierce — An intoxicating blend of body horror and midnight movie madness, reminiscent of early David Lynch and the splatterpunks at their most sublime. **172 pages $11**

BB-124 "Black Hole Blues" Patrick Wensink — A hilarious double helix of country music and physics. **196 pages $11**

BB-125 "Barbarian Beast Bitches of the Badlands" Carlton Mellick III
— Three prequels and sequels to *Warrior Wolf Women of the Wasteland*. **284 pages $13**

BB-126 "The Traveling Dildo Salesman" Kevin L. Donihe — A nightmare comedy about destiny, faith, and sex toys. Also featuring Donihe's most lurid and infamous short stories: *Milky Agitation, Two-Way Santa, The Helen Mower, Living Room Zombies,* and *Revenge of the Living Masturbation Rag.* **108 pages $8**

BB-127 "Metamorphosis Blues" Bruce Taylor — Enter a land of love beasts, intergalactic cowboys, and rock 'n roll. A land where Sears Catalogs are doorways to insanity and men keep mysterious black boxes. Welcome to the monstrous mind of Mr. Magic Realism. **136 pages $11**

BB-128 "The Driver's Guide to Hitting Pedestrians" Andersen Prunty — A pocket guide to the twenty-three most painful things in life, written by the most well-adjusted man in the universe. **108 pages $8**

BB-129 "Island of the Super People" Kevin Shamel — Four students and their anthropology professor journey to a remote island to study its indigenous population. But this is no ordinary native culture. They're super heroes and villains with flesh costumes and out-landish abilities like self-detonation, musical eyelashes, and microwave hands. **194 pages $11**

BB-130 "Fantastic Orgy" Carlton Mellick III — Shark Sex, mutant cats, and strange sexually transmitted diseases. Featuring the stories: *Candy-coated, Ear Cat, Fantastic Orgy, City Hobgoblins,* and *Porno in August.* **136 pages $9**

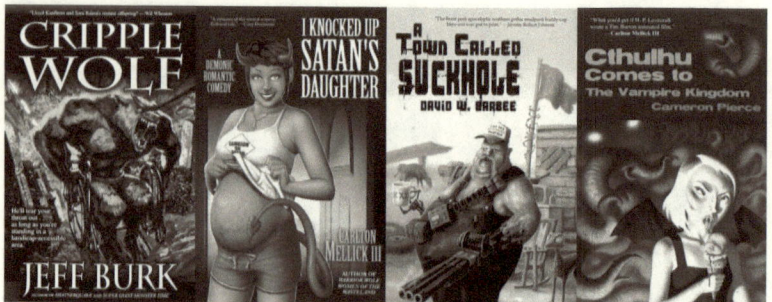

BB-131 "Cripple Wolf" Jeff Burk — Part man. Part wolf. 100% crippled. Also including *Punk Rock Nursing Home, Adrift with Space Badgers, Cook for Your Life, Just Another Day in the Park, Frosty and the Full Monty*, and *House of Cats*. **152 pages $10**

BB-132 "I Knocked Up Satan's Daughter" Carlton Mellick III — An adorable, violent, fantastical love story. A romantic comedy for the bizarro fiction reader. **152 pages $10**

BB-133 "A Town Called Suckhole" David W. Barbee — Far into the future, in the nuclear bowels of post-apocalyptic Dixie, there is a town. A town of derelict mobile homes, ancient junk, and mutant wildlife. A town of slack jawed rednecks who bask in the splendors of moonshine and mud boggin'. A town dedicated to the bloody and demented legacy of the Old South. A town called Suckhole. **144 pages $10**

BB-134 "Cthulhu Comes to the Vampire Kingdom" Cameron Pierce — What you'd get if H. P. Lovecraft wrote a Tim Burton animated film. **148 pages $11**

BB-135 "I am Genghis Cum" Violet LeVoit — From the savage Arctic tundra to post-partum mutations to your missing daughter's unmarked grave, join visionary madwoman Violet LeVoit in this non-stop eight-story onslaught of full-tilt Bizarro punk lit thrills. **124 pages $9**

BB-136 "Haunt" Laura Lee Bahr — A tripping-balls Los Angeles noir, where a mysterious dame drags you through a time-warping Bizarro hall of mirrors. **316 pages $13**

BB-137 "Amazing Stories of the Flying Spaghetti Monster" edited by Cameron Pierce — Like an all-spaghetti evening of Adult Swim, the Flying Spaghetti Monster will show you the many realms of His Noodly Appendage. Learn of those who worship him and the lives he touches in distant, mysterious ways. **228 pages $12**

BB-138 "Wave of Mutilation" Douglas Lain — A dream-pop exploration of modern architecture and the American identity, *Wave of Mutilation* is a Zen finger trap for the 21st century. **100 pages $8**

BB-139 "Hooray for Death!" Mykle Hansen — Famous Author Mykle Hansen draws unconventional humor from deaths tiny and large, and invites you to laugh while you can. **128 pages $10**

BB-140 "Hypno-hog's Moonshine Monster Jamboree" Andrew Goldfarb — Hicks, Hogs, Horror! Goldfarb is back with another strange illustrated tale of backwoods weirdness. **120 pages $9**

BB-141 "Broken Piano For President" Patrick Wensink — A comic masterpiece about the fast food industry, booze, and the necessity to choose happiness over work and security. **372 pages $15**

BB-142 "Please Do Not Shoot Me in the Face" Bradley Sands — A novel in three parts, *Please Do Not Shoot Me in the Face: A Novel*, is the story of one boy detective, the worst ninja in the world, and the great American fast food wars. It is a novel of loss, destruction, and--incredibly--genuine hope. **224 pages $12**

BB-143 "Santa Steps Out" Robert Devereaux — Sex, Death, and Santa Claus ... The ultimate erotic Christmas story is back. **294 pages $13**

BB-144 "Santa Conquers the Homophobes" Robert Devereaux — "I wish I could hope to ever attain one-thousandth the perversity of Robert Devereaux's toenail clippings." - Poppy Z. Brite **316 pages $13**

BB-145 "We Live Inside You" Jeremy Robert Johnson — "Jeremy Robert Johnson is dancing to a way different drummer. He loves language, he loves the edge, and he loves us people. These stories have range and style and wit. This is entertainment... and literature."- Jack Ketchum **188 pages $11**

BB-146 "Clockwork Girl" Athena Villaverde — Urban fairy tales for the weird girl in all of us. Like a combination of Francesca Lia Block, Charles de Lint, Kathe Koja, Tim Burton, and Hayao Miyazaki, her stories are cute, kinky, edgy, magical, provocative, and strange, full of poetic imagery and vicious sexuality. **160 pages $10**

BB-147 "Armadillo Fists" Carlton Mellick III — A weird-as-hell gangster story set in a world where people drive giant mechanical dinosaurs instead of cars. **168 pages $11**

BB-148 "Gargoyle Girls of Spider Island" Cameron Pierce — Four college seniors venture out into open waters for the tropical party weekend of a lifetime. Instead of a teenage sex fantasy, they find themselves in a nightmare of pirates, sharks, and sex-crazed monsters. **100 pages $8**

BB-149 "The Handsome Squirm" by Carlton Mellick III — Like Franz Kafka's *The Trial* meets an erotic body horror version of *The Blob*. **158 pages $11**

BB-150 "Tentacle Death Trip" Jordan Krall — It's *Death Race 2000* meets H. P. Lovecraft in bizarro author Jordan Krall's best and most suspenseful work to date. **224 pages $12**

BB-151 "The Obese" Nick Antosca — Like Alfred Hitchcock's *The Birds*... but with obese people. **108 pages $10**

BB-152 "All-Monster Action!" Cody Goodfellow — The world gave him a blank check and a demand: Create giant monsters to fight our wars. But Dr. Otaku was not satisfied with mere chaos and mass destruction.... **216 pages $12**

BB-153 "Ugly Heaven" Carlton Mellick III — Heaven is no longer a paradise. It was once a blissful utopia full of wonders far beyond human comprehension. But the afterlife is now in ruins. It has become an ugly, lonely wasteland populated by strange monstrous beasts, masturbating angels, and sad man-like beings wallowing in the remains of the once-great Kingdom of God. **106 pages $8**

BB-154 "Space Walrus" Kevin L. Donihe — Walter is supposed to go where no walrus has ever gone before, but all this astronaut walrus really wants is to take it easy on the intense training, escape the chimpanzee bullies, and win the love of his human trainer Dr. Stephanie. **160 pages $11**

BB-155 **"Unicorn Battle Squad" Kirsten Alene** — Mutant unicorns. A palace with a thousand human legs. The most powerful army on the planet. **192 pages $11**

BB-156 **"Kill Ball" Carlton Mellick III** — In a city where all humans live inside of plastic bubbles, exotic dancers are being murdered in the rubbery streets by a mysterious stalker known only as Kill Ball. **134 pages $10**

BB-157 **"Die You Doughnut Bastards" Cameron Pierce** — The bacon storm is rolling in. We hear the grease and sugar beat against the roof and windows. The doughnut people are attacking. We press close together, forgetting for a moment that we hate each other. **196 pages $11**

BB-158 **"Tumor Fruit" Carlton Mellick III** — Eight desperate castaways find themselves stranded on a mysterious deserted island. They are surrounded by poisonous blue plants and an ocean made of acid. Ravenous creatures lurk in the toxic jungle. The ghostly sound of crying babies can be heard on the wind. **310 pages $13**

BB-159 **"Thunderpussy" David W. Barbee** — When it comes to high-tech global espionage, only one man has the balls to save humanity from the world's most powerful bastards. He's Declan Magpie Bruce, Agent 00X. **136 pages $11**

BB-160 **"Papier Mâché Jesus" Kevin L. Donihe** — Donihe's surreal wit and beautiful mind-bending imagination is on full display with stories such as All Children Go to Hell, Happiness is a Warm Gun, and Swimming in Endless Night. **154 pages $11**

BB-161 **"Cuddly Holocaust" Carlton Mellick III** — The war between humans and toys has come to an end. The toys won. **172 pages $11**

BB-162 **"Hammer Wives" Carlton Mellick III** — Fish-eyed mutants, oceans of insects, and flesh-eating women with hammers for heads. Hammer Wives collects six of his most popular novelettes and short stories. **152 pages $10**